CAITLIN COULDN'T BELIEVE HER EARS

"Caitlin," Ginny told her, "Jed spent almost the whole night with Diana—either dancing or talking—and he didn't look as if he was suffering."

Caitlin laughed. "Ginny, you crack me up. You don't really expect me to believe Jed spent a whole night with a *nothing* like Diana?"

"You can believe what you want—but it's the truth."

Caitlin remained on the bed as Ginny took her nightgown and towel and left the room for her shower. Caitlin was furious with Jed. How could he have danced all those dances with Diana? Everyone in the school was probably already talking about it!

It was time for Caitlin to take some serious action!

LOVING

Created by
Francine Pascal

Written by
Joanna Campbell

BANTAM BOOKS
TORONTO • NEW YORK • LONDON • SYDNEY • AUCKLAND

RL 7, IL age 12 and up

LOVING

A Bantam Book / June 1985
2nd printing . . . November 1986

Conceived by Francine Pascal.

Produced by Cloverdale Press Inc.

Starfire and accompanying logo of a stylized star are registered trademarks of Bantam Books, Inc. Registered in U.S. Patent and Trademark Office and elsewhere.

ISBN 0-553-24716-6

Published simultaneously in the United States and Canada

Bantam Books are published by Bantam Books, Inc. Its trademark, consisting of the words ''Bantam Books'' and the portrayal of a rooster, is Registered in U.S. Patent and Trademark Office and in other countries. Marca Registrada. Bantam Books, Inc., 666 Fifth Avenue, New York, New York 10103.

For Danelle McCafferty

1

"That's not a bad idea, Tenny," Caitlin said as she reached for a book from her locker. "Actually, it's pretty good."

"You really like it?" Tenny Sears hung on every word the beautiful Caitlin Ryan said. It was the petite freshman's dream to be accepted into the elite group the tall, dark-haired junior led at Highgate Academy. She was ready to do anything to belong.

Caitlin looked around and noticed the group of five girls who had begun to walk their way, and she lowered her voice conspiratorially. "Let me think it over, and I'll get back to you later. Meanwhile, let's just keep it between us, okay?"

"Absolutely." Tenny struggled to keep her excitement down to a whisper. The most important girl in the whole school liked her idea. "Cross my heart," she promised. "I won't breathe a word to anyone."

Tenny would have loved to continue the conversation, but at just that moment Caitlin announced she'd left her gold pen in French class. Tenny was only too happy to race to fetch it.

The minute the younger girl was out of sight, Caitlin gathered the other girls around her.

"Hey, you guys, I just had a great idea for this year's benefit night. Want to hear it?"

Of course they wanted to hear what she had to say about the benefit, the proceeds of which would go toward a scholarship fund for miners' children. Everyone was always interested in anything Caitlin Ryan had to say. She waited until all eyes were on her, then hesitated for an instant, increasing the dramatic impact of her words.

"How about a male beauty contest?"

"A what?" Morgan Conway exclaimed.

"A male beauty contest," Caitlin answered, completely unruffled. "With all the guys dressing up in crazy outfits. It'd be a sellout!"

Most of the girls looked at Caitlin as if she'd suddenly gone crazy, but Dorothy Raite, a sleek, blond newcomer to Highgate, stepped closer to Caitlin's locker. "I think it's a great idea!"

"Thanks, Dorothy," Caitlin said, smiling modestly.

"I don't know." Morgan was still doubtful. "How are you going to get the guys to go along with this? I can't quite picture Roger Wake parading around on stage in a swimsuit."

"He'll be the first contestant to sign up when I get done talking to him." Caitlin's tone was slyly smug.

"And all the other guys?"

"They'll follow along." Caitlin placed the last of her books in her knapsack, zipped it shut, then gracefully slung it over her shoulder. "Everybody who's anybody in this school will just shrivel up and die if they can't be part of it. Believe me, I wouldn't let the student council down. After all, I've got my new presidency to live up to."

Morgan frowned. "I suppose." She took a chocolate bar out of her brown leather shoulder bag and began to unwrap it.

Just at that moment, Tenny came back, empty-handed and full of apologies. "Sorry, Caitlin, I asked all over, but nobody's seen it."

"That's okay. I think I left it in my room, anyway."

"Did you lose something?" Kim Verdi asked, but Caitlin dismissed the subject, saying it wasn't important.

For an instant Tenny was confused until Dorothy Raite asked her if she'd heard Caitlin's fabulous new idea for a male beauty contest. Then everything fell into place. Caitlin had sent her away in order to take credit for the idea.

It didn't even take three seconds for Tenny to make up her mind about what to do. "Sounds terrific," she said. Tenny Sears was determined to belong to this group, no matter what.

Dorothy leaned over and whispered to Caitlin. "Speaking of beauties, look who's walking over here."

Casually Caitlin glanced up at the approaching

Highgate soccer star. Roger Wake's handsome face broke into a smile when he saw her. Caitlin knew he was interested in her, and up until then she'd offhandedly played with that interest—when she was in the mood.

"And look who's with him!" Dorothy's elbow nearly poked a hole in Caitlin's ribs. "Jed Michaels. Oh, my God, I've been absolutely dying to meet this guy."

Caitlin nodded, her eyes narrowing. She'd been anxious to meet Jed, too, but she didn't tell Dorothy that. Ever since his arrival as a transfer student at Highgate, Caitlin had been studying him, waiting for precisely the right moment to be introduced and to make an unforgettable impression on him. It seemed that the opportunity had just been handed to her.

"Hey, Caitlin. How're you doing?" Roger called out, completely ignoring the other girls in the group.

"Great, Roger. How about you?" Caitlin's smile couldn't have been wider. "Thought you'd be on the soccer field by now."

"I'm on my way. The coach pushed back practice half an hour today, anyway. Speaking of which, I don't remember seeing you at the last scrimmage." There was a hint of teasing in his voice.

Caitlin looked puzzled and touched her fingertips to her lips. "I was there, I'm sure—"

"We were late, Caitlin, remember?" Tenny spoke up eagerly. "I was with you at drama club, and it ran over."

"Now, how could I have forgotten? You see, Roger"—Caitlin sent him a sly, laughing look— "we never let the team down. Jenny should know—she's one of your biggest fans."

"Tenny," the girl corrected meekly. But she was glowing from having been singled out for attention by Caitlin.

"Oh, right, Tenny. Sorry, but I'm really bad with names sometimes." Caitlin smiled at the girl with seeming sincerity, but her attention returned quickly to the two boys standing nearby.

"Caitlin," Dorothy burst in, "do you want to tell him—"

"Shhh," Caitlin put her finger to her lips. "Not yet. We haven't made all our plans."

"Tell me what?" Roger asked eagerly.

"Oh, just a little idea we have for the council fund-raiser, but it's too soon to talk about it."

"Come on." Roger was becoming intrigued. "You're not being fair, Caitlin."

She paused. "Well, since you're our star soccer player, I can tell you it's going to be the hottest happening at Highgate this fall."

"Oh, yeah? What, a party?"

"No."

"A concert?"

She shook her head, her black-lashed, blue eyes twinkling. "I'm not going to stand here and play Twenty Questions with you, Roger. But when we decide to make our plans public, you'll be the first to know. I promise."

"Guess I'll have to settle for that."

"Anyway, Roger, I promise not to let any of this other stuff interfere with my supporting the team from now on."

At her look, Roger seemed ready to melt into his Nikes.

Just at that moment Jed Michaels stepped forward. It was a casual move on his part, as though he were just leaning in a little more closely to hear the conversation. His gaze rested on Caitlin.

Although she'd deliberately given the impression of being impervious to Jed, Caitlin was acutely aware of every move he made. She'd studied him enough from a distance since his recent arrival to know that she liked what she saw.

Six feet tall, with broad shoulders and a trim body used to exercise, Jed Michaels was the type of boy made for a girl like Caitlin. He had wavy, light brown hair, ruggedly even features, and an endearing crooked smile. Dressed casually in a striped cotton shirt, tight cords, and western boots, Jed didn't look like the typical preppy Highgate student, and Caitlin had the feeling it was a deliberate choice. He looked like his own person.

Caitlin had been impressed before, but now that she saw him close at hand, she felt electrified. For that brief instant when his incredible green eyes had looked directly into hers, she'd felt a tingle go up her spine.

Suddenly realizing the need for an introduction, Roger put his hand on Jed's shoulder. "By the way, do you girls know Jed Michaels? He just transferred here from Montana. We've already got him signed up for the soccer team."

Immediately the girls called out a chorus of enthusiastic greetings, which Jed acknowledged with a friendly smile and a nod of his head. "Nice to meet you." Dorothy's call had been the loudest, and Jed's gaze went toward the pretty blonde.

Dorothy smiled at him warmly, and Jed grinned back. But before another word could be spoken, Caitlin riveted Jed with her most magnetic look.

"I've seen you in the halls, Jed, and hoped you'd been made welcome." The intense fire of her deep blue eyes emphasized her words.

He looked from Dorothy to Caitlin. "Sure have."

"And how do you like Highgate?" Caitlin pressed on quickly, keeping the attention on herself.

"So far, so good." His voice was deep and soft and just slightly tinged with a drawl.

"I'm glad." The enticing smile never left Caitlin's lips. "What school did you transfer from?"

"A small one back in Montana. You wouldn't have heard of it."

"Way out in cattle country?"

His eyes glimmered. "You've been to Montana?"

"Once. Years ago with my grandmother. It's really beautiful. All those mountains . . ."

"Yeah. Our ranch borders the Rockies."

"Ranch, huh? I'll bet you ride, then."

"Before I could walk."

"Then you'll have to try the riding here—eastern

style. It's really fantastic! We're known for our hunt country in this part of Virginia."

"I'd like to try it."

"Come out with me sometime, and I'll show you the trails. I ride almost every afternoon." Caitlin drew her fingers through her long, black hair, pulling it away from her face in a way she knew was becoming, yet which seemed terribly innocent.

"Sounds like something I'd enjoy," Jed said, smiling, "once I get settled in."

"We're not going to give him much time for riding," Roger interrupted. "Not until after soccer season, anyway. The coach already has him singled out as first-string forward."

"We're glad you're on the team," Caitlin said. "With Roger as captain, we're going to have a great season." Caitlin glanced at Roger, who seemed flattered by her praise. Then through slightly lowered lashes, she looked directly back at Jed. "But I know it will be even better now."

Jed only smiled. "Hope I can live up to that."

Roger turned to Jed. "We've got to go."

"Fine." Jed nodded.

Caitlin noticed Dorothy, who had been silent during Jed and Caitlin's conversation. She was now staring at Jed wistfully as he and Roger headed toward the door.

Caitlin quickly leaned over to whisper, "Dorothy, did you notice the way Roger was looking at you?"

Her attention instantly diverted, Dorothy looked away from Jed at Caitlin. "Me?" She sounded surprised.

"Yeah. He really seems interested."

"Oh, I don't think so." Despite her attraction to Jed, Dorothy seemed flattered. "He's hardly ever looked at me before."

"You were standing behind me and probably couldn't notice, but take my word for it."

Dorothy glanced at the star soccer player's retreating back. Her expression was doubtful, but for the moment she'd forgotten her pursuit of Jed, and Caitlin took that opportunity to focus her own attention on the new boy from Montana. She knew she only had a moment more to make that unforgettable impression on him before the two boys were gone. Quickly she walked forward. Her voice was light but loud enough to carry to the girls behind her.

"We were just going in your direction, anyway," she called after them. "Why don't we walk along just to show you what strong supporters of the team we are?"

Looking surprised, Roger said, "That's fine by us. Right, Jed?"

"Whatever you say."

Caitlin thought he sounded pleased by the attention.

Quickly, before the other girls joined them, Caitlin stepped between the two boys. Roger immediately tried to pull her hand close to his side. She wanted to swat him off but instead gave his hand a squeeze, then let it go. She was pleased when Diana fell in step beside Roger. Now, Caitlin thought, she could focus on Jed. "There must be a thousand questions you still have about the school and the area. Have you been to Virginia before?"

"A few times. I've seen a little of the countryside."

"And you like it?"

As they walked out the door of the building, Jed turned his head so that he could look down into her upturned face and nodded. There was a bright twinkle in his eyes.

Caitlin took that twinkle as encouragement, and her own eyes grew brighter. "So much goes on around here at this time of year. Has anyone told you about the fall dance this weekend?"

"I think Matt Jenks did. I'm rooming with him."

"It'll be great—a real good band," Caitlin cooed. In the background she heard the sound of the others' voices, but they didn't matter. Jed Michaels was listening to *her*.

They walked together for only another minute, down the brick footpath that connected the classroom buildings to the rest of the elegant campus. Caitlin told him all she could about the upcoming dance, stopping short of asking him to be her date. She wasn't going to throw herself at him. She wouldn't have to, anyway; she knew it would be only a matter of time before he would be hers.

It didn't take them long to reach the turnoff for the soccer field. "I guess this is where I get off," she said lightly. "See you around."

"See you soon," he answered and left.

Caitlin smiled to herself. This handsome boy from Montana wasn't going to be an easy mark, but this was an adequate beginning. She wanted him—and what Caitlin wanted, Caitlin got.

"You going back to the dorm, Caitlin?" Morgan asked.

"Yeah, I've got a ton of reading to do for English lit." Caitlin spoke easily, but her thoughts were on the smile Jed Michaels had given her just before he'd left.

"Somerson really piled it on tonight, didn't she?" Gloria Parks muttered.

"Who cares about homework," Caitlin replied. "I want to hear what you guys think of Jed."

"Not bad at all." Tenny giggled.

"We ought to be asking *you*, Caitlin," Morgan added. "You got all his attention."

Caitlin brought her thoughts back to the present and laughed. "Did I? I hadn't even noticed," she said coyly.

"At least Roger's got some competition now," Jessica Stark, a usually quiet redhead, remarked. "He was really getting *unbearable*."

"There's probably a lot more to Roger than meets the eye," Dorothy said in his defense.

"I agree. Roger's not bad. And what do you expect," Caitlin added, "when all he hears is how he's the school star."

The girls started crossing the lawns from the grouping of Highgate classroom buildings toward the dorms. The magnificent grounds of the exclusive boarding school were spread out around them. The ivy-covered walls of the original school building had changed little in the two hundred years since it had been constructed as the manor house for a prosperous plantation. A sweeping carpet of lawn had replaced the tilled fields of the past; and the smaller buildings had been converted into dormitories and staff quarters. The horse stable had been expanded, and several structures had been added—classroom buildings, a gymnasium complete with an indoor pool, tennis and racketball courts—but the architecture of the new buildings blended in well with that of the old.

"Caitlin, isn't that your grandmother's car in the visitors' parking lot?" Morgan pointed toward the graveled parking area off the oak-shaded main drive. A sleek, silver Mercedes sports coupe was gleaming in the sunlight there.

"So it is." Caitlin frowned momentarily. "Wonder what she's doing here? I must have left something at the house last time I was home for the weekend."

"My dream car!" Gloria exclaimed, holding one hand up to adjust her glasses. "I've told Daddy he absolutely *must* buy me one for my sixteenth birthday."

"And what did he say?" Jessica asked.

Gloria made a face. "That I had to settle for his three-year-old Datsun or get a bicycle."

"Beats walking," Morgan said, reaching into her bag for another candy bar.

"But I'm dying to have a car like your grandmother's."

"It's not bad." Caitlin glanced up at the car. "She has the Bentley, too, but this is the car she uses when she wants to drive herself instead of being chauffeured."

"Think she'll let you bring it here for your senior year?"

Caitlin shrugged. "I doubt if she'll trust me with it. Besides, I've always preferred Jaguars, myself."

Caitlin paused on the brick path, and the other girls stopped beside her. "You know, I really should go say hello to my grandmother. She's probably waiting for me." She turned quickly to the others. "We've got to have a meeting for this fund-raiser. How about tonight—my room, at seven?"

"Sure."

"Great."

"Darn, I've got to study for an exam tomorrow," Jessica grumbled, "but let me know what you decide."

"Me, too," Kim commented. "I was on the courts all afternoon yesterday practicing for Sunday's tennis tournament and really got behind with my studying."

"Okay, we'll fill you guys in, but make sure you come to the next meeting. And I don't want any excuses. If you miss the meeting, you're out!" Caitlin stressed firmly. "I'll catch the rest of you later, then."

All the girls wandered away, except for Dorothy, who remained behind. She was just about to say something when a tall, elegantly dressed, silver-haired woman walked briskly down the stairs from the administrative office in the main school building. She moved directly toward the Mercedes, quickly opened the driver's door, and slid in behind the wheel.

Caitlin's arm shot up in greeting, but Regina Ryan never glanced her way. Instead, she started the engine and immediately swung out of the parking area and down the curving drive.

For an instant Caitlin stopped in her tracks. Then with a wide, carefree smile, she turned to Dorothy and laughed. "I just remembered. She called last night and said she was dropping off my allowance money but would be in a hurry and couldn't stay. My memory really *is* bad. I'll run over and pick it up now."

As Caitlin turned, Dorothy lightly grabbed Caitlin's elbow and spoke softly. "I know you're in a hurry, but can I talk to you for a second? Did you mean what you said about Roger? Was he really looking at me?"

"I told you he was," Caitlin said impatiently, anxious to get Dorothy out of the way. "Would I lie to you?"

"Oh, no. It's just that when I went over to talk to him, he didn't seem that interested. He was more interested in listening to what you and Jed were saying."

"Roger's just nosy."

"Well, I wondered. You know, I haven't had any dates since I transferred—"

"Dorothy! You're worried about dates? Are you crazy?" Caitlin grinned broadly. "And as far as Roger goes, wait and see. Believe me." She gave a breezy wave. "I've got to go."

"Yeah, okay. And, thanks, Caitlin."

"Anytime."

Without a backward glance, Caitlin walked quickly to the administration office. The story about her allowance had been a fabrication. Regina Ryan had given Caitlin more than enough spending money when she'd been home two weeks earlier, but it would be all over campus in a minute if the girls thought there was anything marring Caitlin's seemingly perfect life.

Running up the steps and across the main marble-floored lobby that had once been the elegant entrance hall of the plantation house, Caitlin entered a carpeted, homey-looking office. She smiled warmly at Mrs. Forbes, the dean's secretary.

"Hi, Mrs. Forbes."

"Hello, Caitlin. Can I help you?"

"I came to pick up the message my grandmother just left."

"Message?" Mrs. Forbes frowned.

"Yes." Caitlin continued to look cheerful. "I just saw her leaving and figured she was in a hurry and left a message for me here."

"No, she just met on some school board business briefly with Dean Fleming."

"She didn't leave anything for me?"

"I can check with the part-time girl if you like."

"Thanks." Caitlin's smile had faded, but she waited as Mrs. Forbes stepped into a small room at the rear.

She returned in a second, shaking her head. "Sorry, Caitlin."

Caitlin forced herself to smile. "No problem, Mrs. Forbes. It wasn't important, anyway. She'll probably be on the phone with me ten times tonight."

As Caitlin hurried from the main building and set out again toward the dorm, her beautiful face was grim. Why was she always trying to fool herself? She knew there was no chance her grandmother would call just to say hello. But nobody would ever know that; she would make certain of it. Not Mrs. Forbes, or any of the kids; not even her roommate Ginny. Not anyone!

2

By the time Caitlin entered the old brick girls' dormitory and jogged quickly up the stairs to her second-floor room, she was in perfect control once more. Her roommate, Ginny Brookes, was still out riding, and Caitlin dropped her knapsack on the chair beside the antique writing desk in the corner.

All the furniture in the moderately sized room was the best money could buy. Mrs. Ryan wouldn't allow her granddaughter to "suffer" with Highgate's standard room fare. Although it wasn't unheard of for some of the girls to make their rooms more homey with their own furniture, Caitlin and Ginny were the only students who could boast of a professionally decorated room.

A thick, pale blue carpet covered the floor and matched the custom-made drapes that fluttered in the breeze from the open double windows. The antique mahogany bookcase underneath the windows housed both Caitlin's and Ginny's books as well as a new stereo. The lacy eyelet spread that covered Caitlin's old spool bed was strewn with bright pastel pillows, which were often scattered over the floor as cushions for visiting friends. The decorator had chosen oil paintings for the walls, but the girls had removed them and replaced them with posters, which covered nearly every inch of wall space.

Unzipping her knapsack, Caitlin pulled out a notebook and pen, sat down on the edge of the bed, and began scribbling notes for the beauty contest. She was so engrossed, she didn't hear the door open. She jumped when Ginny called out, "What are you doing here?"

"Huh?" Caitlin stared at her roommate dumbly.

"I thought you had a tennis date with Terry."

"Oh! I forgot all about it." She shrugged. "Well, too late now. I'll talk to him tomorrow."

"He'll be angry, but I bet he'll ask you out again, anyway." Ginny piled her own books on the bed and spoke over her shoulder in awe. "You're really too much! You break dates all the time, and you still have nearly every boy in the school drooling over you."

Caitlin's popularity was something she took for granted, actually, and at the moment she wasn't interested in hearing Ginny go on about it. "I can't help it if boys like to be with me. Besides, Terry will understand. He knows I'm busy. Anyway, we're only friends."

"I wonder if he thinks that's all you are," Ginny said mildly. "You could set him straight, you know. You'd hurt his feelings a lot less if you told him the truth."

"But I want to be his friend."

Ginny gave an exasperated sigh. "The point is that he's interested in more than that."

"Come on." Caitlin laughed. "Why the big deal about Terry? I've told him he's not the only boy I go out with."

"Well, I think he's a nice guy and you shouldn't treat him that way."

"Hey," said Caitlin. "Are *you* interested in Terry?"

"No, of course not!"

"So what's the big deal? Anyway, I've got something really exciting to tell you!"

"Oh?" Ginny draped her tall, angular frame across her bed. Two barrettes drew back her light brown hair from her sharp-featured face in a practical, though not very becoming, way.

"What's up? Should I guess?"

"You never will."

"Bet I can." Ginny's hazel eyes shone with excitement. "This new guy—the one from Montana—you started checking him out the minute he set foot in Highgate, and now you've got a plan for how you're going to catch him."

"Ginny! I don't know why I put up with you. That wasn't what I was going to say at all! I was going to tell you about my plan for the student council fund-raiser!" Caitlin leaned back on her elbows and smiled. "But since you've brought up the subject . . ."

"Aha!"

"I did meet Jed today. There was an instant

connection between us. I could *feel* it. I just mentioned casually that I like to ride, and he said he'd really like to come along sometime. We talked about the dance this weekend, too," Caitlin added casually, twirling her pen in her fingers.

"I'll bet." Ginny looked anything but surprised.

"There's no question he's interested—*very* interested."

"It figures," Ginny said. "And apart from the fact that he's not bad to look at, he's smart. He really seems to know where he's going and what he wants."

"How would you know all this?"

"He's in my English class," Ginny explained. "And now you're going to ask me why I didn't tell you."

"I am not. I've learned all I need to know about Jed Michaels, at least for now."

"Did you know he's Emily Michaels's cousin?"

"Emily?" Caitlin sat up straight. "You're kidding! How'd you find out?"

"Jed was talking to Charlie Imari, who sits next to me in English, and I overheard what they were saying."

Caitlin was silent for a moment. "Hmmm. Emily Michaels. She's kind of cute with all that curly hair. She's a really decent rider, too, but she hangs around with such boring people." Caitlin tapped the end of her pen lightly on her cheek. Her blue eyes narrowed. "I've ridden with her a couple of times, and we talked a little, but I always thought she was a little too"—she shrugged a shoulder

—"*dull*, to fit in with our group. But maybe I ought to give her another chance."

"What are you planning now?"

Caitlin looked at Ginny with innocent amazement. "Why, nothing. Why would you think that? You just reminded me that we've kind of left Emily out of the action. But listen, all this talk has gotten me sidetracked. I wanted to tell you about my idea for our fund-raiser. It's absolutely incredible. I can't believe I thought of it myself!"

"Yes, you can."

But Caitlin hadn't heard Ginny. She rushed on excitedly. "We're going to have a male beauty contest—"

"What?"

"A male beauty contest. Isn't it a great idea? We'll get the guys up onstage in gag outfits and have them do a little talent number and strut their stuff. At the end we'll give out some funny prizes—something like gaudy plastic flowers, some glittery sequined crowns—"

"Oh, cute!" Ginny looked up to the ceiling, then shook her head. "I can just see all those hairy legs in high heels. Count me out."

"What do you mean? Come on, Ginny. It's going to be the best fund-raiser we've ever had here. And I'd really planned on your helping us. I could never arrange it all without your organizing talent. After all, you've run a couple of horse shows by yourself."

"That was different."

Caitlin's mouth puckered into a tiny pout. "Oh, come on, Ginny. We need you."

"I'll think about it."

"I'm having a meeting here about seven tonight. Wait until you see how excited everyone is about it."

Ginny sat up and stretched. "Since you've already arranged the meeting here, I don't suppose I have any choice. In the meantime, I've got some homework to do. Have you seen my poetry book?"

"Yeah, it's over there next to the stereo."

As Caitlin went to the small refrigerator in the corner of the room and Ginny sat down at her desk, there was a knock on the door.

"Who is it?" Caitlin called.

"Mrs. Chaney. I have a message for you, Caitlin."

"One second." Caitlin placed a can of soda on her desk, then opened the door. Mrs. Chaney, the housemother, handed her a folded piece of paper. "A message from your grandmother. She stopped by earlier."

"Oh." Caitlin blinked in surprise. "Sure. Thanks, Mrs. Chaney."

While Caitlin had been talking, the older woman had been glancing quickly around the room. "Well, it's certainly nice to see how neatly you girls keep your room."

"No thanks to me," Ginny said and laughed. "Caitlin goes around picking up after me half the time."

Caitlin shrugged. "Habit, I guess. I like things to look nice."

Mrs. Chaney smiled. "Good for you. I'll let you

girls get back to your homework. We'll see you at dinner."

"Bye."

As the door closed behind their housemother, Caitlin unfolded the note. So, her grandmother *had* left her a message, after all. Hoping that this time the message might be different from the ones her grandmother usually sent, Caitlin began to read. She sighed. The message was typical of Regina Ryan: no nonsense, and to the point.

> I'll be sending Rollins with the car for you Friday afternoon. The national miners' union heads will be joining us for the weekend. They are expecting to meet my granddaughter. This is a very important affair for me. Be sure to dress accordingly.
>
> Grandmother

Caitlin understood too clearly the unstated message: Once again the union people were making demands on her grandmother's mining company, and Regina needed to impress them with her image as doting grandmother and guardian. Still, Caitlin thought, her grandmother *did* want her there, and that meant something.

"Bad news?" Ginny's concerned voice startled Caitlin.

Quickly she folded the note, composed her features, and gave Ginny a wide smile. "Oh, no, of course not. I was just surprised."

"You looked upset to me."

"No, no. Grandmother's having an unexpected party this weekend, and she wants me to come.

Some people I've wanted to meet for the longest time will be there. Isn't it great?"

"But the fall dance is this weekend!" Ginny exclaimed.

"This is so much more important." With a quick movement of her head, Caitlin flipped her hair off her shoulder. "We'll have lots of other dances here, anyway."

Ginny looked doubtful. "I suppose you can't get out of going to your grandmother's, but you'll miss your chance to put the moves on Jed Michaels."

Caitlin ignored her. "I have practically the whole year ahead of me," she said cheerfully.

But as Caitlin turned from her friend and started back toward the bed, her expression was troubled. True, after two years of rooming together, Ginny knew her better than anyone else in the world. But even Ginny didn't know what life at Ryan Acres was really like. All the kids at Highgate envied Caitlin's life with her fabulously rich and powerful grandmother. Not that the majority of the student body wasn't wealthy, but few had homes to compare with the luxurious old Virginia manor house on the Ryan estate. Few of her friends had been exposed to as much travel and as many of the niceties of life as Caitlin had. Caitlin wanted the other kids to believe her life was glamorous and perfect—and she wouldn't allow the tragic loss of her parents to spoil this image of perfection.

She'd made a point of stoically telling anyone who asked, that her mother had died while giving birth to her and that her father had been killed in

an accident not long before. As a result, her grandmother had brought her up from infancy. Part of
what she told people was true. But on threat of
death, she wouldn't reveal the whole story.

Her grandmother spoke of the past tragedy with
curt bitterness and always went out of her way to
remind Caitlin that her father had deserted her
after she was born. When Caitlin's mother, Regina
Ryan's cherished only child, had died giving birth,
Mrs. Ryan had felt obligated to raise Caitlin. She
had provided her with everything money could
buy but had denied her the one thing that would
have cost her nothing—her love.

As Caitlin sat down on the edge of the bed, she
crumpled her grandmother's message into a tight
ball in her hand. She *was* disappointed about the
dance. But like an actress in a drama, she'd play
the dutiful granddaughter while the rest of her
friends were having a great evening.

Promptly at seven, the girls began filing into
Caitlin and Ginny's room. Tenny Sears and Gloria
Parks were the first. Both grabbed pillows from
Caitlin's bed and placed them on the floor.

"Hi, Caitlin." Tenny beamed. "Thanks for inviting me tonight."

"Sure." Caitlin barely glanced up from the desk
where she was working on her list of ideas for the
contest.

"Oh, hi, Ginny," Tenny added, looking toward

the bed. Ginny was sitting with her back propped against the wall, leafing through *Horse and Rider*.

Ginny grinned. "Hi, Tenny."

"Morgan will be here in a minute," Gloria added. "She had to make a phone call. Have you got anything to drink?"

"Sure, there are sodas in the fridge," Caitlin answered. "Get me one, too—a diet Coke."

"Hey, you guys," Gloria said with a secretive smile as she handed around the sodas, "you'll *never* guess what I heard just before we came over! No, maybe I shouldn't say."

"Go ahead," Ginny said, from behind her magazine. "We know you're dying to tell us."

"Spit it out, Gloria," Caitlin demanded.

"Okay. I was talking to Mary Dwight this afternoon, and she'd just gotten a letter from Lauri Halston. Remember her? She's up at Smith this year."

"How could we forget last year's senior queen?" Caitlin muttered sarcastically.

"Anyway, Lauri got a letter from Madge Pouchard last week. Remember how Madge wrote us all the end of this summer saying how she was loving Europe so much that she'd decided to do her junior year at that Swiss finishing school?"

"Sure. How does she like it?" Ginny asked.

"She's not there." Gloria's voice dropped conspiratorially, although it was clear from her expression she was bursting with the importance of what she had to say.

"No? Where'd she go?" Tenny asked, even though she'd never met Madge.

Gloria threw her a look. "That Swiss school story was just a cover-up. Madge never intended to come back. Dean Fleming kicked her out at the end of the term last year!"

"You're kidding!" Caitlin's full attention had been caught by Gloria's last words, and swinging around in her seat at the desk, she began to smile slyly. "How interesting."

"Coming from you that's an understatement," Gloria said, "after some of the things Madge said about you last year."

"We all know Madge and Caitlin didn't get along," Ginny said quietly, "but why did she have to leave?"

"Mrs. Chaney found a couple of bottles of Southern Comfort in her room. Now she's enrolled in some dinky public school near her hometown."

"Anyone jerky enough to let Chaney catch them with booze deserves to be kicked out."

"Oh, come on, Caitlin," Ginny put in.

"It serves her right!" Caitlin flared. "I'm not about to feel sorry for someone who called me a shallow, self-centered flirt."

Ginny shook her head as Morgan burst into the room with Dorothy on her heels. "Sorry we're late! What did we miss?"

"Nothing but a little gossip," Caitlin said mildly. "Grab a pillow and a soda."

"What gossip?" Morgan stepped around Gloria and Tenny and climbed up on the bed. "Could it be the same thing I just heard. About Madge?"

"You got it," Caitlin said, dismissing the story

and taking charge. "Okay, you guys. We can talk later. Right now we've got a lot of business to take care of. I've made a list of some of the stuff we should get going on for the beauty contest. I thought each of you should head a committee. Who wants publicity?"

"I'll do it," Dorothy volunteered. "I did a lot of work on the school paper back at Miss Porter's."

"One down. I'll do recruiting myself."

"Figures." Ginny stifled a laugh. "Sorry, I couldn't help myself. I told you, Caitlin, that this beauty contest wasn't my kind of thing."

"Good. I'll put you at the head of the cleanup committee."

"No, you don't!" Ginny glared. "You know how I hate picking up messes. Give me something behind the scenes—the bookkeeping, printing up the tickets and programs."

"Okay. Ginny's got all of that." Caitlin gave her roommate a malicious grin. "Now, someone for stage decorations and props."

Morgan raised her hand.

The meeting progressed until nearly ten o'clock, with Caitlin firmly in control. By the time they all departed for their respective rooms, the beauty contest was in the process of becoming a reality.

As Caitlin slid under the covers an hour later, she called over to Ginny, who was already curled up in her own bed. "Listen, Ginny, are you going to the dance?"

"I don't know," Ginny mumbled groggily. "Why?"

"I think you should. I hear it's going to be great."

"You know I don't like dances."

"You'll love this one. They've got a terrific new group playing."

"No kidding. Well, maybe I will. I haven't got anything else to do, anyway."

"Ginny?"

"Yeah?"

"While you're there, if you think of it, could you check on Jed occasionally?"

"Fooled again."

"Thanks, Ginny. You're a real friend."

3

Caitlin paused a second to catch her breath before she rounded the corner near the science rooms. She wanted to be sure she'd be in the hall when Jed's biology class let out. Caitlin was thankful the hall was nearly empty. The few kids she saw called and waved greetings, but she smiled back distractedly, in a way that wouldn't encourage anyone to stop and talk.

Her breathing normal again, she ran a hand through her hair, then casually stepped around the corner. She was in no hurry now. Her next class was a study hall, which she usually spent in the library.

A few students were filing into the classroom, but no one was leaving. Could she have missed Jed?

Stopping at the water fountain across from the biology room, Caitlin leaned over to take a drink. As she was rising, she turned and saw Jed step into the hall. He was glancing down at a paper in his hands. Just as he was passing the fountain, he looked up and saw Caitlin.

He smiled and stepped over to her.

"Well, hi!" She gave him a dazzling smile. "This is a surprise."

"How're you doing, Caitlin?"

"Pretty well. How about you?"

"Not bad. I was just talking to Dr. Blake about an idea I had for a project in advanced biology. He seemed to like it. He gave me some papers to read that would tie in. Where are you heading? I'm off to English myself."

"I'm on my way to trig," Caitlin lied glibly, feeling perfectly safe since the trigonometry class-room was the last along the hall. "So what's this idea you have?" she asked.

"A study on animal behavior and changes in the environment. Living on the ranch, I've had a lot of chances to observe wildlife. I'd like to do some real research now."

"That sounds like a big project! Good luck. Dr. Blake's not easy to impress."

"We'll see how it goes."

Caitlin took a lock of her long hair and twirled it around her fingers. "Speaking of projects, I don't know if you heard us telling Roger about the student council fund-raiser yesterday. I've come up with this idea"—her voice grew sweetly troubled— "but I'm kind of worried."

"Why?"

"Because I'm not sure how the rest of the kids in school are going to like it. We can't afford a flop— we want to make some money for the scholarship fund." She hesitated, then suddenly glanced up at him, a bright expression on her face as though an idea had just occurred to her that instant. "You know, I hadn't thought of it before, but what we need is a guy's opinion! You're the perfect one to ask. You're new here and won't think about doing things the way we've always done them before!"

"Okay, try me."

"Well, every year the student council does something to raise money. Until now it's always been stuff like raffles or fairs, but I want to make this year's fund-raiser the best that Highgate's ever had." Caitlin's eyes sparkled with excitement. "The idea I came up with—oh! Class is about to start, and it's going to take too long to explain." Her voice dropped in disappointment. "Darn, and I wanted to hear what you think!"

Jed was gazing at her with interest. "Well, I have some free time after soccer practice this afternoon. Maybe we could get together then."

Caitlin hesitated for the briefest instant, savoring her triumph. Her plan was working perfectly. Then she spoke thoughtfully. "I was only going down to the stables to groom Duster, my horse. But I hate to bother you. You've probably got a thousand things to do."

"Nothing I can't put off. Besides, you've got me curious now. Why don't I meet you at the stables? I've been wanting to take a look around there, anyway."

"Great! If you don't see me in the paddock, come into the stables. Duster's stall is the third on the right."

He nodded, then gave her a big grin. "We'd better run, or we'll both be late to class."

"Yeah, you're right!" Caitlin started off down the hall, then looked back over her shoulder. "See you later! And thanks."

She had to force herself not to go skipping off down the hall in elation. After a brief glance behind to be sure Jed was gone, she glided right past the trigonometry classroom, through the side exit of the science and math building, and out into the early autumn sunshine. Maybe she'd go to the library after all. Studying was the furthest thing from her mind, but she could spend the next forty-five minutes very profitably planning the course of her meeting with Jed later that afternoon.

As she hurried out of the classroom building after French, Caitlin had only one thing on her mind—going to her room and making herself as irresistible as possible for Jed. As much as she liked the way her jodhpurs fit, she was grooming Duster, not riding him. She'd put on a pair of jeans, instead, topped by a teal blue sweater that brought out the color of her deep blue eyes. Casual—that was the image she wanted.

She was mentally debating whether to tie back her hair with a ribbon or a scarf and didn't notice that someone was coming across the lawn toward her. She stopped in her tracks and looked up only when an arm shot out and a hand caught her shoulder.

"Oh! Terry!" she exclaimed. "I was in a daze."

"I guess you were. If I hadn't stopped you, you would've walked right by me."

"Sorry." She pulled her thoughts together and laughed. "Thinking too much, I guess. How are you?"

The blond-haired boy stared down at her, his expression sullen. "I could be better."

"Something wrong?"

"How can you say that after standing me up for tennis yesterday?"

"Oh, my God! Oh, Terry, I don't believe I did that. How could I have forgotten?"

"I stood there waiting for half an hour."

"I've just been so busy! Any my grandmother came by the school in the afternoon—"

"Look, I know you see other guys, but I'm beginning to think you see me only when you've got nothing better to do."

"That's not true." She sounded hurt. "How could you say that?"

"Easily, when I've been stood up."

She looked directly into his eyes. "Terry, you know how much I like you. I'd never deliberately miss a date with you. It's just that things have been so hectic! I feel so pressured."

"I'm not pressuring you into anything. I just don't like—"

"It's not *you* who's pressuring me." Caitlin dropped her shoulders. "It's everyone else. Everybody wants me to do something."

Terry's angry expression softened a little, and he shifted his weight from one foot to the other. "Yeah, I suppose I can understand." Then he brightened. "Well, what are you doing now? Why don't we play a couple of sets of tennis this afternoon?"

Caitlin sighed. "This isn't working out for us at all. I have an English lit paper due, and I haven't even finished all my reading for it."

"Couldn't you take a half hour off? We could get in one set."

She shook her head sadly. "I'd better not. I'm kind of worried about my English grade."

"You? You made dean's list all last year."

"I know, but so far this semester I haven't had as much time for studying."

Terry sympathized. "You really are pushing too hard."

"Mmmm," Caitlin acknowledged. "I guess I'm going to have to ease up." She sighed dramatically. "But I hate to see you miss out on tennis because of me. I'm sure you can find another partner if you want to play this afternoon. What about Ginny?"

"Ginny?" Terry blurted out, thrown off guard.

"Yeah. She's a great player. She'll probably beat you!"

"Well, maybe I could ask her," Terry said skeptically.

"She'd really be thrilled."

"My good deed for the day, huh?"

"Just a suggestion," Caitlin said lightly.

Terry frowned. "Well, if you really think so. Where is she?"

"Probably at the library."

"I'll head over that way." Terry stared down at her. "And I'll see you soon?"

"Just as soon as we both have free time. I promise."

With a wave, Terry started toward the library in the main building, and Caitlin sauntered to the dorm, a satisfied smile on her face. The stables and tennis courts were on opposite sides of the campus. There was no chance of either Terry or Ginny seeing her and Jed. At the thought of Jed, she quickened her pace. It was going to be a perfect afternoon. She'd made certain of that!

4

"You love to have your back scratched, don't you?"
Caitlin cooed as Duster reached his head around
and rubbed his muzzle on her arm. She had him in
crossties in the stable and was brushing a curry
comb in a circular motion over his gleaming black
coat.

Duster nudged her again. "You know I have
another apple in my pocket. Sorry, big boy, but
you're just going to have to wait until I'm done
grooming you." She turned to the bench behind
her and exchanged the curry comb for a brush.

"If I were him, I don't know if I'd want to wait."

Caitlin nearly jumped in surprise. Quickly she
swung around to see Jed approaching in jeans and
a rugby shirt. He was obviously fresh from the
shower because his dark hair was damp.

"You scared me!" Caitlin cried.

"Sorry." Duster's ears pricked forward as Jed
stepped closer. He paused before the horse and
rubbed a hand over his muzzle. "Hi, there, fella."

He spoke in a soothing tone. "You're a beauty, aren't you." Jed ran his hand over Duster's neck and appraised the animal's lines. "How old is he? About four or five?"

"He's a four-year-old. I got him at auction as a yearling. My grandmother wasn't keen on him—he was pretty gawky then—but she said if I was willing to break him and train him, I could have him."

"You broke him yourself?"

"With a little help from one of our stable hands. Duster's still a little green, but he's a natural fencer. I'm entering him in the fall show."

Caitlin watched as Jed stepped under the crossties and continued to inspect Duster. "Do you hunt, Jed?"

"Sure, but not the gentlemen's hunt you have here in the East. When we head out into the Montana woods after deer, we just pack a bedroll and a rifle. But I've done a little jumping."

"That's all you need! If you can take a clean fence and stay in the saddle, you can hunt."

"Once the soccer season's over, I'll have more time to give it a try."

Duster was getting restless, and Caitlin reached into her pocket for an apple. She walked forward, stepped under the crossties, and offered the treat to Duster. She now had a clear view of Jed again. "How did practice go?"

"Not bad," Jed answered, "but we've still got a lot of work ahead to pull the team together. It's not easy for the rest of the team having a new guy come on after the season's started."

"Why *did* you start late?" Caitlin asked.

"I applied late, and I was first on the waiting list for a cancellation, but one didn't come through till school had started." He looked at Duster. "You want to walk him a little? Looks like he wouldn't mind."

Caitlin wasn't about to pass up the opportunity of walking with Jed and prolonging their meeting. "Sure. That's a great idea! The stable hands are supposed to keep the horses exercised, but they don't always have time."

As Jed released the crossties, Caitlin reached over to grab a lead rope from one of the hooks on the wall.

"Look at his ears perk," Jed noted. "He knows he's getting out. You'd much rather be out there stretching your legs, wouldn't you, boy? I don't blame you."

"I can tell you're used to animals."

It irked Caitlin that Jed seemed to be paying more attention to Duster than he was to her. But she wasn't about to give up yet. As they stepped out into the sunlight, one on either side of Duster's head, Caitlin motioned to the tree-shaded path beyond the paddock. "Let's walk him over there. It's prettier, and it will be cooler for him." The path was also more private. Their conversation was a lot less likely to be interrupted there.

Jed unlatched the paddock gate and held it open as Caitlin led Duster through. After closing it, he rejoined her at Duster's head. They started walking away from the stables.

"He's got a nice, even gait," Jed commented.

"Doesn't he?" Behind her smile Caitlin was fuming. She had to get the conversation onto something besides her horse. "I haven't told you about our plan for the fund-raiser yet."

"I was just going to ask you about that," he said easily.

"When we got so involved in horse talk," Caitlin teased, "I thought maybe you'd decided you didn't want to hear."

"I wouldn't have come all the way out here if I didn't."

His blunt response wasn't at all what she'd expected; she'd expected a little flirtation. Nevertheless, she plunged on. "Well, like I started to tell you, I came up with this idea for a male beauty contest. What I have planned is. . . ." Feeling uncharacteristically off balance and out of control of the situation, Caitlin rushed on with a description of the contest. She was almost breathless when she concluded, "And we'd call out the three runners-up, hand them each a plastic bouquet, and then we'd have Dr. Foster bring out this huge tinsel crown—"

She stopped short as Jed gave a loud laugh.

"What are you laughing at?" she asked, frowning.

Jed only shook his head and continued chuckling.

"You think it's stupid."

40

"No. I think it's great!"

Caitlin sighed with relief.

"I was just picturing some of the guys on the soccer team dressed as girls." Again he gave a loud laugh. "I don't know if you're going to get them to do it, but if you can pull it off . . ."

"Oh, I can get them to do it," Caitlin said assuredly, finally back in control. "But do you think the rest of the kids will like it?"

"Why not? I'd pay five dollars for a show like that. But I'll tell you now, I'm not volunteering to be one of the contestants."

"That's not why I asked you," Caitlin purred. "I only wanted your opinion." She paused. "But you wouldn't consider it at all? Not even for the scholarship fund? Don't you want those poor kids to be able to go to college?"

"Trying to work on my sympathy, huh?"

"Well . . ." She glanced sideways at him.

"I'll be glad to help you out—work backstage, or whatever. But, remember, I'm a cowboy. I have my reputation to consider. Besides, I have bowed legs."

"You do not!"

His cheeks dimpled. "The answer is still *no*."

"Then I'll have to ask Roger."

"So *that's* what you were kidding him about that day we met. I didn't know what was going on. Sounded like you promised him *he'd* be the first to know your plans."

Caitlin tossed her head. "Oh, well, Roger's a nice guy, but being captain of the soccer and basketball teams, he always has to think he's first."

41

"I won't tell him he's not, if you don't. In fact, I'll encourage him to be a contestant."

"You will?"

"It'd take the heat off me."

They'd reached a point in the path where a gate separated the inner Highgate grounds from the lush meadows and woodland beyond. The better riding trails wound through those acres.

"We'd better turn back," Jed said, although he paused at the fence and gazed out at the rolling land beyond. "This is really beautiful." There was almost a wistfulness in his voice. "Kind of reminds me of home."

"Do you miss Montana?" Caitlin asked softly.

"Sometimes. I haven't been away long enough to get really homesick, and I'll be going back there for the Christmas break. I guess I'll always feel a real strong tie to the ranch." He hesitated, deep in his own thoughts. "Well, we'd better get this guy back to his stall. I've got that biology project to get started on tonight."

Caitlin frowned in disappointment, but Jed was turning Duster and didn't see her expression. Their meeting had finally started to go the way she'd planned it, and now he wanted to go back. She sought for something to say that would continue the mood of their conversation, but Jed spoke first.

"You mentioned your grandmother before," he said, walking along, now, beside Caitlin, who held the lead rope. "You must be close to her."

"I live with her." Caitlin smiled. This line of conversation was exactly what she wanted.

"Oh, you stay with her during the school year?"

"No." Caitlin allowed a touch of sadness to enter her voice. She glanced down at the gravel path as they walked. "All the time. My parents are dead."

"I'm sorry." For a brief instant he touched his fingers to her arm. "That's a rough break."

"Well, it happened a long time ago. My father was killed in an accident while my mother was pregnant with me, and my mother . . . well, she died when I was born. So I never knew either of them, except from pictures, but it's still hard. I kind of feel like I'm missing something. You know, all the other kids have families to do things with. . . ." She let her voice fade.

Again Jed touched her arm. "I can understand how you feel." His voice was filled with concern. "Not that I've lost either of my parents, but we've had some real bad problems in the family. My parents were divorced not that long ago. It really tore our family apart." He sighed. "I don't like to think about it. Of course, that's nothing compared to what you've had to deal with."

Caitlin nodded.

"At least my father and I are still close," Jed continued. "And you have your grandmother."

"When she's there."

"I don't understand."

"Oh, she's always off on business. She runs Ryan Mining, you know."

"No, I didn't, but I've heard of the company. Who hasn't? I never thought to make the connection."

"Well, it's all my grandmother's interested in."

"Come on, you've got to be more important to her than a company."

Caitlin glanced up. Her eyelashes held the slightest trace of dampness. "I guess I am. In fact she's having a party this weekend and told me it's important that I come. I think she's having some business people in. There probably won't be anyone my age, but she likes to show me off."

"That can't be the only reason she wants you to come."

"I know. It's just that sometimes she can be so cold, I wonder. Now I'm being silly. I don't mean to cry to you about my problems. I don't usually like to bother people—"

"But you've got to talk to someone once in a while."

Caitlin gave him a brave little smile. "Thanks for listening. I'm kind of disappointed, though, to be missing the dance this weekend."

"Oh, yeah. I'd forgotten all about it."

"Are you going?"

"I guess I'll have to. I told my cousin I'd go with her. But we have a soccer game Saturday afternoon, and I know I'm going to be beat."

"Your cousin?"

"Didn't you know that Emily Michaels is my cousin? I guess I take it for granted people know we're related—because of the last name."

"Now *I'm* the one who didn't make the connection," Caitlin lied. "Emily and I go riding sometimes. She's a great kid. I like her."

"I'm staying with her family—my aunt and uncle—when I'm not here at school. Emily didn't want to go to the dance alone and asked if I minded going along with her and her girlfriend."

"She shouldn't worry about going to the dance alone. Everybody knows everybody else."

"She's a little shy. Either that," Jed added, "or she's worried about *me* meeting people and wants to be sure I go."

"I can't picture you having trouble making friends. You're so easygoing."

Jed laughed. "Well, I'll let Emily think she's giving me a helping hand. She's sure I'm going to pick up and head back to Montana."

"I don't think you're going to do that."

"No, not yet, anyway." He turned his head, and his eyes met Caitlin's. Slowly they smiled at each other. Then the spell was broken by the sound of voices in the stables. Suddenly both of them realized they were almost back at the paddock gate.

Duster nickered, and Jed reached for the latch.

"You don't have to bother bringing him in with me," she said, knowing there would be no chance for private good-byes inside. "Besides, I know you want to get started on that science project." She paused, then looked up at Jed with a gentle smile. "I really liked talking to you. Thanks for listening, and for all your advice."

"For what it was worth."

"It's been a nice afternoon."

He nodded. "It has. It's been fun." He studied

her face in silence, and Caitlin felt a thrill of excitement. She wondered what was going through his mind.

"I'll see you soon?"

She nodded happily at him.

"You can bet on it," she whispered under her breath, as he walked away.

5

Caitlin spent the next morning on a high. She felt secure about Jed and was already thinking ahead to their first real date. But she had no intention of pushing him. Better not to let Jed think she was too eager. There'd probably be no time to talk to him anyway, since she'd be leaving for home right after her last class. Monday would come soon enough, and if he acted like the other boys she knew, by then he'd be camped in front of her dorm door, anxious to see her.

She stepped into the lunch line at noon and, because she was in such a good mood, piled her tray with food: a hamburger, french fries, a piece of chocolate cake, an apple, and a glass of milk. She'd probably never eat it all, but she felt hungry and, unlike some of the other girls, she'd never had to worry about dieting. The exercise she got from riding and tennis kept her five-foot-eight-inch figure slim.

Caitlin left the serving area and stepped into the huge, rectangular cafeteria that had once been the formal dining room of the original plantation house. The elegant graciousness of the architecture had been retained, from the polished hardwood floors to the hand-carved mahogany paneling adorning the walls and large fireplaces at either end of the room. Four crystal chandeliers were suspended from the high, molded plaster ceiling. Their pendants sparkled in the sunlight streaming in through the tall windows, which overlooked the veranda and side lawns of Highgate. The only real change was in the room's furnishings. Instead of the massive central table of old, smaller rectangular tables were spaced in rows from one wall to the other.

Caitlin saw Ginny seated with Morgan at their usual table by the windows and started in that direction. She'd chosen that particular spot at the beginning of the semester because it gave a clear view of the whole room. She'd barely traveled ten feet when she heard her name called.

"Hey, Caitlin! Can't you even say hello?"

She glanced quickly to her right. "Well, Roger." She beamed. "I couldn't believe McGinty had the nerve to throw a spot quiz at us this morning! How'd you do?" Gracefully she moved down the aisle to the table where he was seated with some of the other soccer players. She'd already noted that Jed wasn't with them.

"Don't ask," he grumbled. "I'd hardly opened that history book since the beginning of the term. Why don't you have a seat and join us. Help me forget."

"I can't. Ginny's waiting for me, but I did want to

talk to you." She set her tray down on the table and began eating a french fry.

"You did?"

"Mmmm. Remember that secret we were talking about the other day—about our fund-raiser?"

"Yeah."

"And I told you when we were ready to make it public, you'd be the first to know?"

"You're ready to tell me now?"

"I sure am. Do you want me to tell you in front of these other guys?" She wrinkled her nose playfully. "Or should I whisper in your ear?"

"What's this secret stuff?" Tim Collins called out. "What makes Roger so special? You can tell all of us."

"Well, he's the captain of the team."

"Big deal."

Roger was now blushing with embarrassment. "You might as well let them hear, too," he mumbled.

Caitlin glanced slowly around the group of boys. "Okay. But on one condition. Before I tell you about this incredible idea I have, you all have to swear to take part."

"Take part in what?" Matt Jenks asked.

"I can't tell you that until you swear."

"Come on, Caitlin—" Tim pressed.

"I'll bet Roger will swear. I was counting on him, anyway, to be the star of our show." She glanced at him from the corner of her eye.

"Star of the show?" Roger looked interested. "Well, no idea you came up with could be that bad. Sure, I'll swear."

"And the rest of you?" Caitlin persisted.

"Okay . . . yeah . . ." The others agreed a little more reluctantly.

Caitlin waited half a second, then said cheerfully, "We're having a male beauty contest."

"What!" Roger froze with his sandwich halfway to his mouth.

"Oh, no." Tim Collins lowered his face into his hands. "What have we gotten ourselves into?"

"Don't look so horrified," Caitlin said breezily. "Everyone's going to love it—and love you guys for doing it! Besides, you promised."

Roger was shaking his head in bewilderment. "Me? In a beauty contest?"

Cliff Richards snorted. "That's really scraping the bottom of the barrel."

"Can it, Cliff!" Roger shot back. "You're in it, too."

"Let's see," Caitlin continued merrily. "There are five of you here. We'll need at least seven more contestants—a dozen would be good. We're having a meeting Monday night at seven in the gym. I'll tell you all the details then."

"I'd like to hear a few right now!" Tim called out.

"I haven't got time." Caitlin popped a french fry in her mouth, then picked up her tray. "But what I need you to do for me before Monday is to find seven more guys and have them at the meeting."

Roger groaned, but Tim chuckled maliciously. "You can bet on it. If I'm going to get up and look like a fool, I want as much company as I can get!"

Caitlin flashed them an angelic smile. "Oh, guys, you're great!" Before any of them had a chance to get in another word, she sailed away toward her own table.

As Caitlin set her tray down and hung her knapsack on the back of her chair, Ginny stared over at her. "What was that all about?"

Caitlin sat down and took a big bite of her hamburger. "I just signed up five volunteers for the beauty contest."

"So, you pulled it off," Ginny said with surprise.

"Did you think I wouldn't?"

Ginny was about to respond, but Caitlin was staring across the room, her attention caught. Ginny looked over in the same direction. "Well, well, look who's here."

"Who?" Morgan stopped eating and twisted her head around. "Oh, so if it isn't Jed Michaels, Highgate's new boy idol. Who's he with? Emily?"

"Hmmm," Caitlin mused, studying the trio who had just entered the dining room and were standing with their trays, looking for a table. "And that new girl—the one on scholarship—I can't remember her name."

"Diana, I think." Ginny took a bite of her sandwich.

"Wonder why he's hanging around with those two?" Morgan asked.

"Emily's his cousin," Caitlin said absently, taking another bite of her hamburger. Her thoughts were focused on Jed and his companions.

"I didn't know that. Where does Diana come in?"

"Now I remember," Caitlin spoke almost to herself. "I've seen her and Emily together."

"Right! She's real quiet, hardly has anything to say. Spends most of her free time baby-sitting for Dr. Foster to earn extra money."

"So I've heard." Caitlin wrinkled her nose in disdain but continued watching the girl. She was decidedly plain, nothing special at all. Her best feature, Caitlin decided, was her long, sandy blond hair. Her figure wasn't too bad—a little on the skinny side—but her clothes! Definitely old-fashioned, and the colors she was wearing were all wrong. They washed her right out.

"Jed sure seems interested in what she has to say," Ginny said.

"Don't be absurd." Morgan laughed. "What could he see in her? She's a little mouse!"

"Well, I've always preferred mice to cats, myself. Can I get you a saucer for your milk, Morgan?"

Morgan swung around. "Now, just wait a second, Ginny!"

"Cut it out, you guys," Caitlin said calmly, taking a swallow of milk. But she'd noticed Jed's attentiveness, too, and didn't like it one bit. He obviously hadn't seen her sitting on the far side of the room. If he had, he would have come over. Well, she'd remedy that on her way out of the dining room. This Diana was certainly no threat to her plans.

"If you two are so worried," Ginny couldn't resist adding, "why don't you invite them to sit down over here?"

"Who said anything about being worried?" Caitlin spoke carelessly as she returned her attention to her meal. In a moment she added nonchalantly,

"Jed told me how Emily's going out of her way to make him feel comfortable at Highgate. He's just being nice and having lunch with her and her friend."

"Too late to ask them, anyway." Morgan finally turned back to her own tray. "They found a table." Then she regarded Caitlin. "You seem to know an awful lot about Jed. When did you find all that out?"

"The other day when we were walking him and Roger to practice. And I've run into him a couple of times since."

"Oh."

Ginny was struggling to hold back a laugh.

"What's so funny?"

"Nothing, Morgan." Ginny began pushing back her chair. "I'm going to go. I'll probably see you before you leave, Caitlin."

"Aren't you coming to the pep rally?" Morgan asked.

"I'll see. Actually, I think I'm safer being with my horse." Ginny cast a sidelong glance at Caitlin. She was a little upset over having been forced to play tennis the other day with Terry, especially because he'd acted as if he were doing her a favor. It was only later she'd discovered Caitlin had used her to keep him company while she talked to Jed.

"What did she mean by that?" Morgan asked as Ginny walked away.

Caitlin shrugged. "Don't ask me. Ginny can be strange at times." She put the plate with the slice of chocolate cake on it on Morgan's tray. "Take this. I can't eat it." She grabbed the apple and stood up.

"Think I'll take a walk around outside before class." It wasn't a coincidence that the door to the side lawns was right next to the table where Jed was sitting. "I'll talk to you later."

After picking up her knapsack, she sauntered off, waving and calling out to a couple of people as she weaved through the cafeteria. When she was a few feet away from Jed's table, she glanced over. Jed was watching her, and she smiled as though caught by surprise.

"Oh, hi! I didn't even see you here. Hi, Emily."

"Hi, Caitlin." Emily gave a friendly wave. "Looks like you've already met my cousin."

"I sure have." Caitlin totally ignored Diana. She stepped a little closer to their table. "Did you get your science project started?"

"Just barely," he said. "Matt decided to serenade me with his latest songs."

"What did you think?"

"The music's not so bad, but his voice is a little flat."

"I know what you mean," Caitlin agreed. "By the way, I talked to Roger." Her eyes twinkled. "He and four of the guys on the soccer team are all ready to be contestants. You'll probably hear all about it later."

"What are you two talking about?" Emily asked.

"It's too long to go into now. I'll let Jed tell you," Caitlin said. "I haven't seen you down at the stables lately."

"No, the last couple of weeks have been hectic." Emily sighed.

"Well, let's go riding again soon. What about next week sometime?"

"Sure."

"How about Wednesday afternoon?"

"Great. I don't have anything planned."

"Okay. I'll see you then." She glanced back at Jed. "Why don't you come with us?"

"I have practice. But if you two can wait till I'm done, I'd like to come along."

"I don't mind. Do you, Emily?"

Emily shook her head. "I've been telling him to try out the stables. He's a real good rider."

"Then it's set. I'd better get going and let you finish your lunch. See you Wednesday, if not before. Good luck at the game tomorrow, Jed. I'll be thinking about you guys."

"And you have a good weekend, too." His words held a silent message, which Caitlin understood perfectly.

"I'll try," she said, looking back at him with those penetrating eyes that seemed to signal the words, *but I'd rather be here with you.*

At home Caitlin tried her best to keep up her cheerful spirits. Soon after she arrived at Ryan Acres she reveled in a deliciously long bubble bath in the sunken tub in the bathroom adjoining her bedroom. It was a luxury even as exclusive a boarding school as Highgate couldn't provide for its students. The bath relaxed her and gave her the breathing space she needed to forget about the many goings-on at school and to concentrate on the immediate matter at hand—being a gracious hostess for her grandmother's guests.

After her bath Caitlin donned a long Chinese silk robe and stood inside her walk-in closet, trying to decide on a suitable outfit to wear to the cocktail party. None of her pants outfits—even her dressy satin and silk ones—would do. Regina Ryan frowned upon slacks at social gatherings. After rejecting several dresses her grandmother had bought for her during a recent shopping trip in Georgetown, Caitlin finally settled on a magenta-and-pink chiffon dress she'd bought in Rome the previous summer.

Admiring herself in her floor-length mirror, Caitlin knew she'd made a wise choice. The dress's straight, classic lines made her slim legs look long and elegant, and the daring V neck made her appear older than not-quite sixteen. *Grandmother will be pleased*, she told herself.

By the time Caitlin was ready to make her appearance, a number of guests had arrived. She recognized a few of them: Malcolm Turner, the head of Underwood Mining; Bob Lowery, the president of the miners' union; and a man whose name she couldn't remember who headed the local union at her grandmother's West Virginia mines. Smiling brightly, she greeted each of them warmly, in the poised and friendly way her grandmother had taught her so well.

"Where's your grandmother?" Mr. Turner asked her, taking a bite out of the hors d'oeuvre he held in one hand.

"She probably had to take a phone call. I'm sure

she'll be here in a minute," Caitlin told him, looking in the direction of the double mahogany doors that led to the hallway and her grandmother's study.

She had barely said the words when Regina Ryan strode purposefully in through the double doors, a smile pasted on her slim, patrician-looking face. The tall woman was dressed in a muted gray sheath dress accented only by a diamond necklace given to her many years earlier by her late husband. The look was simple but decidedly elegant. She appeared to float across the room to Caitlin and made a grand show of giving her charge a warm hug.

Everyone's attention was focused on Regina Ryan, which made her announcement slightly unnecessary: "Attention everyone. Have you all met my granddaughter, Caitlin? She's been kind enough to interrupt a very busy schedule at Highgate to join us this weekend." Still holding Caitlin by the arm, Mrs. Ryan slowly nudged her toward one of the corners of the immense living room. "I'd like to talk to you for a minute."

No "hello." No "how are you?" Caitlin thought bitterly. Just a simple, cold directive. She didn't like the accusing tone in her grandmother's voice, either. "What's wrong?"

"Where did you get that dress?" she hissed.

"You remember. I picked it up in Rome last summer. What's the matter? Don't you like it?"

"It's too flashy. Go take it off and put on something more appropriate. This isn't one of your school parties."

Caitlin felt herself stiffen with humiliation. Nothing she did seemed to please her grandmother. "Would my brown cowl neck be better?" It was the plainest dress she could think of.

Regina Ryan smiled again. "Much. Now go along and change. And, Caitlin, when you come back down, don't forget to tell Mr. Lowery about your fund-raiser."

"Don't worry, Grandmother, I won't," Caitlin said. But her grandmother was already gone, greeting some guests who'd just arrived.

Slowly, without turning back, Caitlin marched back up the carpeted steps, her spirits totally deflated. It was going to be a long, long weekend.

6

"How was your weekend?"

"Fabulous!" Caitlin was sitting on her bed with her knees drawn up to her chin and her arms wrapped around her legs. She'd arrived back at the dorm only a few minutes earlier but, instead of unpacking, had plopped down on the bed. "Grandmother really put on some party—tennis, riding, champagne on the lawn before dinner—the works."

"Sounds terrific. Why do you look so down?" Ginny commented, closing the door behind her. She flopped down on her own bed.

"Guess I'm tired. It was hectic, and it was all adults."

"I thought you said your grandmother was inviting a bunch of people you wanted to meet?"

Caitlin didn't respond to the comment. "I wish you'd been there—what a great weekend for riding!"

"Your grandmother didn't invite me."

"But she wouldn't have minded. She really likes you. She's always asking about you."

"Is she?" Ginny seemed pleased. "I guess I do get along pretty well with her. She knows her horses, and we can talk."

Caitlin made a sour face, then pushed the thought of her grandmother aside and spoke more cheerfully. "You haven't told me what went on here this weekend."

"I was waiting for you to ask," Ginny said, grimacing. "I don't think you're going to like it."

Caitlin suddenly sat up straighter and stared at her friend. "Well?"

"I went down to the rally for a little while. Emily and Diana came by themselves. Afterward, the guys went over to talk to Morgan and her bunch. Most of the girls were waiting for Jed to come over, too, but he never did. He waved, but he went right up to Emily and Diana and left with them."

"Oh, that's nothing to worry about. If he'd gone off with Dorothy, I might be upset, but Emily and Diana? Besides, I told you Emily's been trying to show him around."

"There's more." Ginny swung around to a sitting position. "Jed came to the dance with Emily and Diana."

"He told me he was going to. Emily didn't want to go alone. He was just doing her a favor."

"Oh, really?" Ginny widened her eyes skeptically. "Is that what he told you?"

"Okay, smartie, why else would he come with her?"

"Because he's getting very interested in her friend Diana."

"Ginny! Don't be a jerk. Just because he walked into the dance with her and Emily—"

"Caitlin, he spent almost the whole night *with* Diana—either dancing or talking—and he didn't look as if he was suffering."

Caitlin laughed. "Ginny, you crack me up. You really don't expect me to believe Jed spent a whole night with a *nothing* like Diana?"

"You can believe what you want"—Ginny shrugged—"but it's the truth."

Caitlin was shaking her head. Jed with Diana? How hilarious! Yet a small fear nagged away in the back of Caitlin's mind: Ginny wouldn't have made it up; she never lied or exaggerated. "It doesn't mean anything," Caitlin said aloud. "He was probably bored. And what was Emily doing all this time?"

"Dancing with Terry."

"He has some nerve! He asked *me* to go to the dance with him!"

"After the way you've been treating him, I don't blame him! Besides, if you'd been there, you probably would have been flirting with Jed."

"I don't flirt," Caitlin said indignantly. "You're just saying that because you probably spent the whole night all by yourself."

"No, I didn't," Ginny said airily.

"You're kidding. You were dancing?"

"No, but I was talking to someone."

"Who?"

"I'm not telling you. If I did, you'd start trying to interfere."

"Come on, Ginny," Caitlin pleaded. "You can't

keep a secret from me. Is it one of the juniors? I know—Teddy Cannon! He's always in the library."

"Nope."

"Then Mike—"

"Forget it, Caitlin. When I'm ready, I'll tell you."

Ginny took her nightgown and towel and left the room for her shower. Caitlin remained on the bed. She was furious with Jed. How could he have danced all those dances with Diana? Everyone in the school was probably already talking about it! But more than at Jed, her anger was directed toward this Diana person, whoever she was. If Caitlin had been at the dance instead of suffering through a boring weekend at Ryan Acres, none of this would have happened!

7

Caitlin was just leading Duster from his stall on Wednesday afternoon when Emily hurried into the stables. "Am I late?"

"No, I just got here myself." Caitlin glanced out past Emily. "Where's Jed?"

"He should be here in a minute. He told me he'd be down as soon as he could after practice."

Caitlin relaxed. "We can get the horses saddled in the meantime. I thought Journeyman would be a good mount for Jed. He's strong and a good fencer."

Emily nodded. "Jed can handle just about anything."

"He told me." Caitlin fastened Duster in cross-ties, then followed Emily down the stable aisle to get the other horses.

"I hear you guys had a great time at the dance last weekend." Caitlin spoke the words carelessly, as if she were only making conversation. Her intention was to pry as much information out of Emily as possible before Jed arrived. Except for a few moments out on the soccer field, she hadn't seen Jed since her return and had no idea whether he'd been with Diana since the dance. None of her friends had been able to add to her information.

"We sure did! Too bad you missed it."

"I know. Everyone's talking about it. Ginny said you and Terry danced a lot together."

"I couldn't believe it!" Emily exclaimed. "I've always thought he was cute, but he never paid much attention to me before."

"And your friend Diana had a good time, too?"

"The best. I had a hard time getting her to come—she doesn't feel like she fits in here, what with being here on scholarship and having to baby-sit to help pay her way. Meeting my cousin has been great for her!"

"Oh?" Caitlin unlatched Journeyman's stall door and stepped inside to take the horse's halter and back him out. "She and Jed are seeing each other?"

"Well, nothing serious, but since the dance they've gotten pretty friendly." Emily backed her own mount out of his stall. "I'm happy. I never thought the two of them would hit it off."

"Neither did I." Caitlin used all the skills she had picked up at the drama club to hide her disgust. "They seem so different."

Emily continued. "Not really. Diana's actually a lot like Jed's younger sister. She's shy and introverted, too. When their parents got a divorce a couple of years ago, she fell apart, and Jed was great with her."

"Really?" Caitlin's tone encouraged Emily to continue.

"Yeah. Jed's mother was just the opposite. It was pretty obvious when I was a kid and used to go visit my aunt and uncle in the summer that she liked to flirt. She was gorgeous, too—big green eyes and long, dark hair. She always seemed out of place on the ranch. Anyway, two years ago she took off for California with some producer who'd been filming a movie not far from the ranch. None of them has seen her since." A worried expression on her face, Emily suddenly swung to Caitlin. "You won't tell Jed I told you this, will you? He'd have a fit. He never talks about the divorce."

"I'd never say a word!"

"Thanks."

Caitlin waited until Emily had her horse secured. As they walked to the tack room for the saddles, Caitlin's eyes suddenly brightened with a sly twinkle. "I was just thinking, Emily. I know you're busy, but how'd you like to join the student council fund-raiser committee?"

"I don't know what I could do to help."

"Lots of things. You're smart. We could really use you!"

Emily blushed. "If you really think you need me—"

"We do!" Caitlin insisted. "Come to the next meeting, okay?"

"Well, okay," Emily agreed, then grew thoughtful. "It's too bad Diana's always baby-sitting for the Fosters. She'd love to get involved in something like this."

"Oh? Has she done it before?"

"Well, no, but she never has time for the fun stuff at school."

"Yeah, that's too bad." Privately, Caitlin was delighted that Diana would be excluded until it struck her that that might make Jed feel even more sorry for her. "You could ask her, anyway," she added generously. If Diana did join, Caitlin would think of a hundred ways of making her feel uncomfortable.

"Maybe I will. She doesn't have many friends. Just me and now Jed, and Laurence Baxter."

"Laurence?" Caitlin exclaimed. She'd seen the good-looking junior around the stables often. He was nice, but he didn't go out for many of the school activities, and he hung around with a much quieter crowd than she did.

"He was Diana's brother's best friend until her brother was killed in a car accident a few years ago. He's the one who suggested she try for the scholarship to Highgate."

"I thought I heard voices in here." Jed stuck his head around the tack room door.

"Oh, hi, Jed!" Caitlin beamed, wondering how much of their conversation he'd overheard.

"I ran all the way down here thinking I was late, and you guys aren't even saddled up yet," he teased.

"We can fix that." Caitlin laughed. "Here, grab a saddle." She hoisted one in his direction. With a quick step forward, he caught it, and the three of them moved out to the horses.

A few minutes later they'd left the paddock on horseback and were trotting through the gate for the outside riding trails.

Caitlin leaned over to Jed. "How do you like him?"

"So far, so good. He handles nicely."

"Are you going to try some fences with us?" Emily asked.

"I don't see why not—even if the two of you make me look bad."

"That'll never happen!" Caitlin's eyes twinkled. "Emily's told me what a great rider you are."

Confident of her ability and not about to pass up a chance to impress Jed, Caitlin led Duster across the field. Her seat was perfect as Duster ate up the distance across the meadow. She easily circled back to the other two, who were a few strides behind her.

"I'm going to take him over the fence at the end," she called. "Follow me."

"I want to warm up a little more," Emily shouted back. "Wait for us by the stone wall."

Caitlin nodded cheerfully, then reined Duster away and started toward the fence. She knew what an incredible sight she and Duster made when they were flying over a course together. Because she'd trained him herself, their movements were in unison.

She lined up Duster for the fence. As she collected the reins and Duster gathered his strides in preparation, she felt the animal's excitement. How he loved to jump! He loved that soaring sense of freedom as much as she did and was just as exhilarated by it.

Caitlin gauged their approach, mentally counting strides. One, two, she squeezed her legs, and

Duster was up with a powerful leap, clearing the fence with a foot to spare. He landed cleanly and cantered away.

Caitlin crossed half the next field, then turned Duster back. The horse needed no encouragement from his rider and only the barest touches of guidance from her hands and legs to send him soaring again over the fence. As he pounded away from the fence, eagerly snorting and shaking his head, Caitlin pulled him down to a trot. She was anxious to find out what Jed had thought of her expertise.

But it was Emily who spoke up. "Nice jump!" she called. "You could have added a rail, and he still would have gone over."

Caitlin's eyes were bright with her own success. "He's really coming along, isn't he? If he keeps up like this, we'll be sure to take a ribbon in the November show." She looked directly at Jed, expecting to see admiration in his eyes. But he was only studying her, a thoughtful smile on his face.

"Well." She laughed. "What did you think? Ready to give it a try?"

"You really ride him to the inch, don't you." His tone was mild, but the way he accented the words made Caitlin feel as if he thought she'd been pushing Duster just to make an impression.

"Yes, we do work well together, don't we?" she said, choosing to ignore his implied criticism. "Anyway, we're out here just to have fun!"

"I'd say you take it a little more seriously than that."

"Well, sure, when I'm on a hunt course or doing

a show. But not today. Why don't we take the other trail? It's more for pleasure riding, with just a couple of fences. We could talk better anyway."

He continued studying her, his smile unchanged. "Let me try this guy over the fence here first."

"Jed," Emily said in a slightly concerned voice, "I don't know if that's the best fence to start out on since you haven't done a lot of jumping."

Jed had turned his head and was regarding the fence Caitlin had just cleared twice. "Can't be much more than three feet."

"More like three and a half," Emily corrected in the familiar way of a relative. "And not the fence to try on a mount you've only ridden fifteen minutes."

"I know my horses," Jed assured her calmly.

"Yeah, but—"

"I'm going to try him."

Before Emily, or Caitlin for that matter, could say a word, Jed reined Journeyman away and set him to a canter. From the way he easily maneuvered the animal, there was no question that he was in full control. Jed turned Journeyman toward the fence.

"He said he's hardly ever jumped!" Caitlin couldn't help crying.

"But he never brags either, so maybe he's better than even I know," Emily said.

Without being aware of it, Caitlin was holding her breath as Jed drew closer. Would he calculate his strides right? He hardly knew Journeyman or any of the horse's quirks. One second off stride, one stumble, and they'd go through the fence, not over it.

But Jed had him over. He wouldn't win any ribbons with a style like his, Caitlin thought, but the jump was smooth and clean.

Jed was grinning when he pounded up next to the girls and pulled Journeyman to a screeching, cowboy-style halt. "Next I'll teach him how to be a cow pony."

"You were great!" Caitlin said.

"I had a couple of scary seconds. This guy should have told me he likes to throw in an extra step and change lead just before a jump."

"Does he do that?" Caitlin exclaimed. "I've never ridden him. I didn't know."

"It was okay. I pulled him up in time."

"Hey, Cuz." Emily was grinning and holding up a hand with her thumb and first finger joined in a circle, the other fingers extended. "Not bad. Wait till I tell Diana. She's got to let us give her riding lessons now!"

"Oh, Diana doesn't ride? That's too bad," Caitlin noted, her voice heavy with false regret.

"She's scared around horses," Emily said, almost apologetically.

Caitlin's eyes widened in amazement, though secretly she was glad to hear it. Casually she pulled Duster's head up from the grass he'd started to nibble. From the corner of her eye, she glanced at Jed, who was watching her again with an expression she couldn't define. "Let's do the other trail. We can cut out down the valley and make the loop back." Caitlin knew that route would take them about an hour.

"Perfect," Emily agreed. "There're some fences on that trail I want to try, and there's lots of open riding, too. What do you say, Jed?"

"Lead the way." He pulled up on Journeyman's reins so that the horse was waiting for his command.

They had ridden for about fifteen minutes, their concentration on the winding trail, watching for hidden fences. During those minutes, Caitlin had subtly let Emily take the lead while she paced herself beside Jed. There was no need to talk, she felt, as they ducked beneath autumn-colored branches, the horses' hooves making a muffled clopping sound over the fallen leaves on the trail. She glanced over at Jed occasionally.

He seemed happy, though silent, and, as much as she wanted to find out just what was going on between him and Diana, she didn't want to disturb that peace. Where the path was narrow, they took turns clearing the fences; where it was wide, they jumped together. For someone who hadn't done much jumping, Jed impressed Caitlin with his technique. He was so natural, moving with his horse as if he were part of it. It had taken her hours and hours to achieve that same relaxed expertise. Although she knew that she could out-jump him any day of the week, she had no desire to show off. It was fine that they were together; for the moment, it was all she wanted.

Caitlin finally felt the need to speak. She cocked her head and looked at him. "Do you like it? Is it a lot different from the West?"

"In some ways." He was still staring straight ahead. "These hills are nothing compared to Montana, and of course, we've got the open spaces where you could ride for twenty minutes flat out and never hit much but a prairie-dog hole or two."

"How'd you end up in Montana?"

"Oh, our branch of the Michaels family went west before the Civil War." He smiled to himself. "We've got shipping and horse breeding here, and cattle breeding there. Guess it all mixes."

"My family was in shipping, too, when they first settled near Williamsburg. Then they were plantation owners, then mine owners when the market for crops went bad. Now my grandmother's got her own horse-breeding farm."

"And runs Ryan Mining?"

Caitlin nodded. "We sure come from the same kind of backgrounds. And you're a Virginian, too, even if you were born in Montana!"

While Jed had been staring at the path ahead of them, Caitlin found herself unable to take her eyes off him. She was so absorbed admiring his straight, ruggedly handsome profile that she'd totally forgotten one of the worst fences in the trail—a stream followed by a patch of four-foot-high brush.

Jed had neatly cleared it by the time Caitlin caught sight of the imposing obstacle. Quickly, in the instant that followed, she instinctively grabbed Duster's reins and pulled hard. But it was too late, and Caitlin knew it. She gritted her teeth in preparation for what she knew was coming.

Just like the image that played across her mind, Duster's left leg splashed in the water. Caitlin squeezed him hard, but the horse was off stride, and he scraped his knees on the brush. He stumbled on the rocky path and nearly fell when he landed. It was only Caitlin's years of riding experience that kept him on all fours and her from taking a terrible fall.

As Caitlin concentrated on steadying the horse, Jed dismounted quickly and, holding Journeyman's reins, went to check Duster's legs. "I think he'll be okay," he said seriously.

"You're sure?" Caitlin looked worried as she looked down over Duster's shoulder. "He really rapped his right knee."

"There's a small scratch, but it *is* hard to tell if he bruised anything." Jed suddenly turned and looked up at her. "How are you?"

"Fine . . . fine . . ." Her voice was still breathless. She should have been watching for that fence. She couldn't believe her carelessness!

"You look pretty shaken."

"I am! But if anything's happened to Duster—"

"It would have been a lot worse if you'd broken your neck."

The concern in his eyes as he looked up at her left Caitlin speechless. He was really worried about her!

In the next moment Emily came trotting back down the trail. "I thought I'd lost you guys. Oh! What happened?"

Jed turned to his cousin. "Duster nearly took a fall."

"It was my fault." Caitlin shook her head. "I was

talking and wasn't paying attention. Duster's scratched his leg."

"I think we ought to walk him back," Jed added. "In fact"—he glanced at his watch— "I have to head back anyway. I didn't realize we'd be out so long."

He walked around Journeyman, brought the reins over the horse's head, and remounted. "What's the easiest way?"

"Straight across the next field, then there's an old dirt road," Caitlin volunteered.

"You have a lot of homework to get done?" Emily asked Jed.

"No. I promised Diana I'd stop by the Fosters late this afternoon. She's piled under and has to study for an exam. I'm going to help her out."

Caitlin couldn't believe her ears. He said it so casually, as if there weren't the least thing wrong with his leaving her and rushing off to another girl! And here she'd just nearly fallen and broken her neck! It was a good thing that Caitlin was a few steps behind Jed and Emily as they started off so they couldn't see the incredulous expression on her face.

Despite the sarcasm in her words, she forced her voice to be calm and cheerful. "I'm sure Diana can get her studying done by herself. I thought she was here on scholarship."

"Keeping an eye on the Foster kid doesn't leave much time for concentration," Jed answered without looking back.

"And you help her out by doing her baby-sitting for her?"

"I don't mind. I like kids."

Caitlin was gripping her reins so tightly that Duster shook his head in protest. Instinct prevented her from saying what was on her mind. Instead she muttered, "Well, if I'd taken on a baby-sitting job, I wouldn't shove it off on somebody else."

Now Jed did glance quickly back at her. "Have you had to do a lot of baby-sitting, Caitlin?"

"No, I haven't, but—"

"Then I don't think you have any idea how hard it is for her," he snapped back. "Her parents don't have much money, so she's got to work, and she's got to keep her grades up or lose her scholarship."

"That's true," Emily sympathized. "The rest of us don't have any idea what it's like. She's always so tired. Not that she complains."

Caitlin's teeth were clenched. Jed seemed almost angry at her. She had to get back on his good side. "When you put it that way, I understand now. I had no idea it was so hard for her."

Jed sighed. "I suppose a girl like you wouldn't understand."

It took all of Caitlin's willpower not to explode. What did he mean by "a girl like you," saying it as if there were some awful evil attached to being born rich. In any event, she had to find some way to shift the conversation away from Diana.

"Actually, it is a good thing we're heading back early," she said. "I'd forgotten how much I have to do tonight: French homework, an English paper, and some organizing for the benefit. And I want to make sure Duster's leg is cleaned and bandaged before I put him away."

She had Jed's attention again. He turned around in the saddle. "How's he doing? Pulling up lame at all?"

Caitlin had been too furious to pay much attention to her horse, but she wasn't about to admit it. Quickly she glanced down at Duster's leg. "Hmmm, he seems to be favoring his other leg. I'll check him out when we get to the stable."

For an instant Jed looked at her face before swinging forward again. It was enough to make Caitlin wonder if she'd misjudged the situation. Maybe all Jed felt was pity for Diana. Emily had said they were only friends. She'd said, too, that Diana was a lot like his sister. And he *had* seemed very worried when she and Duster had nearly taken that fall.

Her expression grew cunning. She'd get him yet. It was only a matter of time.

8

Caitlin found it almost impossible to concentrate as she sat down at her desk to do her homework. Duster's injury was worse than she'd originally thought. By the time she'd returned to the stables, his leg had begun to swell. The trainer feared it was a bad bruise and warned her to stay off Duster for the next few weeks. That meant he wouldn't be able to compete in the big horse show in November.

But as much as she cared about Duster and as disappointed as she was about having to miss the show, Caitlin's mind kept wandering back to the afternoon's ride. She went over every detail a thousand times. She'd been having such a wonderful time with Jed until he'd mentioned Diana. Why did he have to ruin everything?

"You're doing more daydreaming than homework tonight," Ginny said as she crossed behind Caitlin to get to the refrigerator.

"I was thinking about something."

"Wild guess: Does his name begin with a J?" Ginny paused as she reached for the refrigerator door. "You haven't said much about your date today."

"It was fine. But I was thinking about something else. I want to have a party at Ryan Acres next weekend."

Ginny popped open the can of Sprite in her hand. "I'll come."

"You'd better. I'll have tennis and lots of riding, maybe even a picnic lunch on Saturday."

"Who else are you inviting?"

"Oh, Morgan, Dorothy, Gloria, Roger, Terry, Jill and Steve from drama club, Emily and Jed—"

"I'm beginning to get the picture."

"What picture?"

Ginny took a sip from her soda. "I'll bet you're not inviting Diana."

"Why should I?" Caitlin shrugged. "She's not a friend of mine."

"And since when did Emily become one of your buddies?"

"She happens to be nice. I got to know her better when we were riding today. She wants to work on the fund-raiser, too."

"If you're using this party as a way to get to Jed, you're crazy."

Caitlin gazed at Ginny in amazed innocence. "Why do you think things like that? All I want to do is have a fun party. Listen! Why don't you invite this secret boyfriend of yours?"

Ginny only smiled. "He's not my boyfriend. We're just friends."

Caitlin's eyes twinkled with mischief. "Invite him anyway. I'm dying to know who he is."

"I'll think about it." Ginny laughed and walked over to her bed.

Caitlin put her pen to the paper in front of her, but all she managed to write in the middle of her notes was "Jed."

Caitlin called the next fund-raiser meeting for that Friday night. At quarter to seven her friends began filing into the gym. She'd gotten there early with Ginny and Dorothy, who had decided to work together on the programs and publicity.

"I've got a question, Caitlin," Dorothy called across the circle of folding chairs they'd set up to one side of the gym. "Do you want me to hit the local papers with the announcement?"

"Of course! We want to get as many people here as we can. If you need names, my grandmother knows the publishers."

"Yeah, give me a list. I'll get all the information together, and we can just mail it out."

"Hand deliver it. It will be more impressive."

Dorothy stared at her. "How? You know I haven't got a car."

Caitlin smiled as an idea bloomed in her mind. "Don't worry. I'll talk to Brett Perkins. He'll do it." She looked down at the papers in her hands again.

"You mean Brett with the classic MG?"

"The same." Caitlin glanced up. "I'll tell him to call you at the dorm."

"Really?"

Caitlin nodded, mentally adding another name to her invitation list. She saw Roger and some of the other boys who had agreed to be contestants coming through the door. Putting down her pad and pen, she went over to meet them.

"I'm glad you're early, Roger. I wanted to talk to all you guys before the meeting started." Caitlin glanced around the group. "Jed's not with you?"

"I haven't seen him."

One look at Roger's scowling brow and Caitlin realized her mistake. She reached out and patted his arm. "It doesn't matter anyway whether he's here. He's not one of the contestants. Let's go over to the side where the others won't bother us. What I wanted to talk to you guys about was your costumes. Gloria's in charge of that committee, and she'll help you out if you have trouble getting an outfit together. I'd like to stick pretty close to the theme—"

"We wanted to mention that to you, Caitlin." Tim Collins ran a hand through his short blond hair, but his expression was stubborn. "None of us is really keen on dressing up like girls."

"Oh?"

"Well, we know it's for a good cause and all that stuff. But I, for one, don't want to look like a total fool."

"Yeah, I feel the same way," Billy O'Hare muttered. Some of the others nodded in agreement.

Caitlin turned to the team captain. "And what do you think, Roger?"

There was a flush of discomfort on his handsome face. "I agree."

"No problem," Caitlin said gaily. "We'll just change the costumes. How's this? You can wear whatever you want as long as it's different and kind of funny. You know, like an English butler, a rock star, or farmer. And if someone decides to dress as a girl, that's okay, too. I'll bring it up at the meeting"—she glanced at the clock on the wall— "which should be starting right now. Grab a seat, guys."

She stepped away to weave through the crowd of other committee members. In her mind's eye, she could see her grandmother's approving nod. When she was a few feet from her chair, Morgan came hurrying over.

"Caitlin, I'm having trouble getting the materials for the backdrop. Ginny won't let me go over budget—"

"No problem. Borrow some of the old sets from the drama club. There's got to be something we could use."

"Why didn't I think of that? Thanks, Caitlin."

Caitlin turned away to start the meeting. Just as she was about to climb up on her chair to get everyone's attention, she saw Jed walk into the gym with Diana.

For an instant Caitlin's face fell; then she took a deep breath, forced her mouth into a smile, and got up on the chair. "Okay, you guys!" she yelled. "Meeting's in session. Find a chair."

There was a moment of bedlam and a quick

scramble for seats, but within three minutes Caitlin had the meeting running smoothly. There was nothing she liked better than being in charge. It didn't matter whether it was a scholarship fund-raiser or a pep rally—as long as she was the star.

As she announced the change in costumes, settled some squabbles over committee duties, and listened to suggestions from the floor, she kept her eyes away from where Jed and Diana were sitting on the far side of the circle. She'd deal with that situation when the meeting was over.

By eight o'clock, all the major problems had been solved, and the committee was ready to break up into individual groups. As everyone started moving into separate corners, Caitlin motioned to Jessica Stark and spoke to her quietly. "Diana Chasen's here for the first time tonight. Why don't you get her on your committee if she's interested? I know you need someone else."

"Boy, do I ever! I'll go talk to her."

As Jessica started walking over to Jed and Diana, Caitlin searched for Emily. She finally found her talking with Ginny. Caitlin tapped her shoulder.

"So what do you think, Emily? Have you decided what committee you want to be on?"

Emily nodded. "Ginny and Dorothy could use me."

"Great!" Caitlin laughed. "I just wanted to tell you I'm having a party at Ryan Acres next weekend. We can ride, play tennis—all kinds of stuff. I'd like you to come."

"I'd love to!"

"I'll be inviting a whole group. Tell Jed, too, though I'll be talking to him myself."

"Great! I've heard so much about Ryan Acres from my father. He and your grandmother do a lot of business together, you know."

"Sure. I've heard her mention his name. Oh, we're going to have a great time, Emily." She lowered her voice to a conspiratorial whisper. "I've invited Terry."

"Hey, Caitlin!" someone called from across the room.

"I hear my name. I'll talk to you again long before next weekend."

Emily nodded, and Caitlin turned to see who had been calling her name. She saw Tim waving a hand. He was standing in the middle of a group of the soccer players—and Jed was with them. It couldn't have been more perfect. She hurried over.

"What's up?" She laughed as she squeezed between two of the guys to get to Tim. She was very aware that Jed was standing to her right watching her.

"A couple of questions. Now about these costumes—who's supposed to get them?"

It took her only a few minutes to reassure Tim and give him the answers he wanted. But she was glad he'd called her over. Now she would have the perfect opening to pull Jed aside, invite him to her grandmother's, and see where their conversation led.

But when she turned to face him, he was gone. Quickly she broke out of the cluster of boys and looked around the gym. He was walking over to

Diana, and as she and Jed met, Caitlin saw her shake her head in answer to some question he'd asked.

Damn! Caitlin thought. Had the mousey girl decided she didn't have the time to work on the fund-raiser? Or was she just antisocial? Caitlin knew she couldn't go over and find out now. She had no intention of letting Diana get included in the invitation to Ryan Acres.

As she stood debating what to do, Jed and Diana left the gym together.

Although she still hadn't managed to corner Jed alone and invite him, during the next two days Caitlin plunged ahead with the arrangements for the upcoming weekend. She knew her grandmother wouldn't mind the extra guests. As long as Caitlin's friends were well behaved, Regina Ryan would allow her granddaughter free rein around the estate. She was too busy to take a more active interest.

On Monday Caitlin was heading toward her English class with Morgan and Gloria when she saw Jed standing outside one of the classroom doors farther up the corridor. He was looking at some papers in his hands.

Breaking away from her friends, Caitlin increased her pace and moved to the side of the hall so that her path would lead her directly, although seemingly accidentally, to Jed. She prepared her expression. She'd seem innocently surprised to see him, then would give him one of her warmest smiles.

When she was only a few feet away, her lips ready to call out a greeting, Diana Chasen stepped out of a classroom into the hall. She and Jed exchanged a warm look, and Jed stuffed his papers into his notebook. It was clear he'd been waiting for Diana, and Caitlin stopped dead in her tracks.

She watched them as they started slowly up the hall, walking so close together that their arms touched. Jed leaned over to say something to Diana, and she looked up at him adoringly. She answered him, and he nodded back, his expression soft.

Disgusting! Absolutely disgusting, Caitlin cried to herself in fury. *How can he fall for that puppy-dog act?*

Caitlin was so beside herself that when Bobby Matthews, a sophomore, hurried up to her and offered to walk her to her next class, she agreed readily.

Early the next morning, as she left the breakfast line in the dining room with her usual orange juice and English muffin to eat out on the front lawn, Emily came hurrying over to her.

"I'm glad I saw you."

"Hi, Emily. Come outside and eat with me." Caitlin didn't add how glad she was to see Emily, too.

"I've already finished, but I'll walk out with you."

"You all set for this weekend?"

"Oh, yeah, I'll be there. And I talked to Jed. He said he'd come, too."

Caitlin suddenly felt much happier. "Did he? Great! We've got some terrific horses in the stables—I've got one in mind for him to try out. I've been trying to ask him myself, but I've just been so busy—and I haven't run into him."

"Don't worry, he wasn't upset that I asked him for you."

"I'd still like to talk to him. What's he been up to?"

"I don't know." Emily seemed uncertain. "After our ride Wednesday, I decided I needed to get back in shape and try for one of the winter shows. I spent most of the weekend practicing jumps."

"How'd you do?"

"I'm getting there again. Anyway, I saw Jed only for a couple of minutes Saturday morning. He and some of the soccer team guys were heading out for a ten-mile jog, then they were going to climb the mountain and have dinner in town at the coach's house."

So, Caitlin thought, *no wonder I haven't seen Jed anywhere on campus until yesterday's brief glance.* "I've got about a dozen people coming," she told Emily.

"Listen, Caitlin, would you mind if I brought someone else along, too? I know it's kind of late to ask."

"Who?"

"Diana."

Caitlin nearly crushed the orange juice container in her hand.

"She doesn't have to baby-sit this weekend and asked me to do something with her. I hate to leave her here all alone on campus. She hasn't met a lot of people yet."

"She isn't exactly going to be alone—there'll be about three hundred kids here with her."

"Oh, I know, but since she's been here, she hasn't had time to do anything fun. Getting away for the weekend will be great for her."

Caitlin frowned. "Not that I wouldn't love to have her, but my grandmother said I could have only twelve people, and I'm not sure we could find her a bed."

"Oh, she can share with me. I wouldn't mind. That is, if your grandmother doesn't mind an extra person," Emily pleaded. "Actually, Jed said he would be just as happy staying on campus and letting Diana go in his place. He said he had lots of stuff he could do here."

Caitlin's throat tightened in near desperation. The whole point of her party had been to get to know Jed better. Yet it suddenly seemed that the only way she could get him there was to let Diana come, too. What other excuses did she have? Her grandmother really wouldn't have cared if she had two dozen guests. And the question of an extra bed was laughable—there were twelve double bedrooms at Ryan Acres.

"I'll talk to my grandmother. I'm sure I can talk her into another guest. Tell Jed there's no reason for him not to come."

"Oh, thanks, Caitlin." Emily gave her a quick hug. "Diana will be so happy."

Forget Diana, Caitlin fumed inwardly. What was happening to her carefully wrought plans? Why was everything working out wrong?

She clenched her fists, determined to turn the

situation to her advantage. She wasn't ready to give up yet—not by a long shot! There were still other ways to make Jed look at her instead of Diana, and a weekend of seeing unsophisticated Diana among the privileged and popular Highgate crowd should do the trick.

Caitlin smiled slyly to herself. Perhaps Diana's coming wasn't such a bad thing after all.

9

At a quarter past four on Friday afternoon, Caitlin, large canvas bag slung over her shoulder, walked slowly down the brick path toward the front entrance of the main building. Rollins would be meeting her by the stairs. With most of her guests arranging their own transportation, only Emily, Diana, and Jed would be riding to Ryan Acres with her.

The three others were already waiting by the curb. Caitlin's eyes rested for a moment on Diana. The nervous-looking girl was dressed in a beige wool skirt and pullover. Her sandy hair was pulled back in a ponytail, and she wore no makeup. Her appearance was neat, but her outfit lacked style and sophistication.

Jed stood beside Diana almost protectively, which irked Caitlin no end. But he was as handsome as ever in a green sweater that emphasized his eyes, and well-fitting tan corduroys that accentuated his long legs. For a moment Caitlin felt something inside her go soft, but that softness quickly disappeared at the sight of Jed continuing to stand so close to Diana.

Still, Caitlin forced a smile as she approached them. "All ready to go, I see," she called out.

"We sure are!" Emily called back excitedly. "I just hope we haven't brought too much luggage."

"No problem. The car has a huge trunk." As Caitlin stopped and lowered her canvas bag to the sidewalk, Jed nodded to her in greeting. He seemed perfectly relaxed and at ease.

"It was nice of you to invite us, Caitlin. The weekend sounds like a lot of fun."

"I'm so glad you're coming!" Although Caitlin's words could have been intended for all of them, she riveted her blue gaze directly on him. His eyes met hers, but she could read no reaction in them. In a moment he looked down at Diana.

"Have you met Diana, Caitlin?" His tone was no more than polite.

"We've seen each other, but we've never actually been introduced."

They studied each other. Caitlin, beautiful and magnificently poised in her brand-new indigo jump suit; Diana, clean-cut and unassumingly sweet.

Caitlin was the first to speak, using all her acting abilities to keep the dislike and jealousy from her tone. "Hello, Diana. Nice to meet you."

Diana extended her hand and smiled. "It's good to meet you, too. I want to thank you for inviting me."

"You're welcome." Caitlin accepted the girl's hand and resisted the urge to grind her teeth in disgust at Diana's shy goodwill. Was Diana so confident of Jed that she had no qualms about welcoming a beautiful adversary? "I hope you'll have a good time," Caitlin lied with a winning smile.

"Oh, I will. It's been awhile since I was able to get away and do things with other kids. The Fosters are wonderful to work for. I just wish I had a little more free time."

At that moment Regina Ryan's sleek, black Bentley rolled around the corner of the Highgate drive and slowed to a stop in front of them. Caitlin turned from Diana and raised her hand in greeting as Rollins, Mrs. Ryan's loyal, middle-aged butler/chauffeur, climbed from behind the wheel.

"How are you today, Miss Ryan," he called cheerfully.

"Just great, Rollins. You're right on time."

The portly, gray-haired man stepped around the rear of the car to open the trunk, then came to collect their bags. "Nice weekend for a party. Your grandmother's at the house, miss. Said she'd see you there."

As Rollins loaded the bags in the trunk, Caitlin glanced at Diana. The girl had taken an unconscious step closer to Jed, and from her expression, she seemed awed by the car. Rollins came around to open the rear door, and Caitlin smiled at Jed.

"Jed, would you mind taking the front seat? I think you'd be more comfortable up there than on the drop seat."

He laughed. "You're right about that. I want to talk to Rollins anyway about this car. He turned to Rollins. "What year is it?"

"Nineteen thirty-six. Mrs. Ryan's husband had it brought over from England. Of course, that was before my time."

Caitlin motioned Diana into the backseat, then slid in herself between Diana and Emily.

"This is great!" Emily exclaimed as Rollins closed the door firmly behind her. "I feel like I've been transported back into one of those old late-night movies."

"This car is wild," Caitlin agreed. "I always notice people turning around to stare, although my grandmother hardly ever uses it—she'd rather drive herself."

"She's crazy," Emily answered emphatically. "This limo makes my parents' Mercedes look like a Honda."

"Well, I wouldn't go that far, Emily," Caitlin said.

As Emily and Caitlin talked, Diana gazed silently around the interior of the car, then out the window. As Rollins started the car out of the Highgate drive and onto the roadway, Caitlin turned to her. "So, have you brought all your riding gear, Diana? Ryan Acres' stables are terrific, if I do say so myself. I thought we'd all go out tomorrow, then have a picnic lunch on the lawn."

Diana tried to force a bright expression to her face, but the effort was obvious. "Actually, I didn't . . . I don't ride. I've always wanted to," she rushed on, "but we lived in Norfolk when I was growing up, and I never had the chance. But don't worry, you guys go riding. I can keep myself busy and meet you for lunch."

Caitlin's eyes widened in mock surprise. "Oh, I'm sorry, Diana. When I made plans for the weekend, I just assumed everybody'd be riding." Her voice was heavy with forced sincerity. She hoped Emily wouldn't remember that she had told her Diana couldn't ride.

But Emily didn't. She leaned forward and looked over at her friend apologetically. "I was so excited about the riding myself, I forgot that you wouldn't have anything to do, Diana."

"That's okay." Diana smiled in reassurance.

"I have an idea," Caitlin interrupted them. "Not everyone is as crazy about riding as Emily and I are. A couple of the kids I invited from drama club would probably rather play tennis . . . Jill Taylor and Steve Wilson. Do you know them?" She continued on without waiting for Diana's response. "And we can get Jim, one of the stable hands, to play a fourth. He plays with me when I'm home alone, so I can promise you he's pretty good—"

"I don't want to put anyone out," Diana protested, forcing herself to smile. "I'll find something to do. Really. I can take a walk, and I brought along a book that I wanted to read."

"Are you sure?" Caitlin studied Diana with seeming concern, well aware of the closed sliding-glass window separating the front and back seats of the car, which prevented Jed from overhearing a word of their conversation and coming to Diana's aid.

Diana nodded, and Caitlin didn't press her any further. She was satisfied. From the expression on Diana's face, Caitlin knew that she didn't play tennis either and now was feeling completely ill at ease.

Caitlin turned her attention to Emily. "Did I tell you about the horse I've got picked out for you? A big gray named Jester. He's got beautiful gaits and is fantastic over fences. I finished third with him in the Ransom hunter-chase last year."

"You're kidding!" Although Emily had been worrying about Diana, her interest was firmly caught by Caitlin's words.

"You'll like him, and I thought I'd give Black Knight to Terry. He can be spooky at times, but Terry can control him."

Emily nodded, smiling. "Terry's a good rider."

"And I think your cousin will love Challenger. The gelding lives up to his name, but after seeing Jed ride the other day, I think he's perfect for him."

Emily and Caitlin chatted gaily about horses as Diana sat quietly, deep in thought, until Rollins swung the car into the oak-bordered drive of Ryan Acres. They traveled a quarter of a mile under the overhanging trees. On either side of the drive, freshly painted white fences enclosed green pastures, where sleek thoroughbreds grazed contentedly. In the distance the white-columned front of the two-storied manor house made a breathtaking sight. Set on a low hill, the elegant two-hundred-year-old structure seemed to reign over the lands surrounding it. Just in front of the house, where the drive made a wide curve, a fountain splashed down into a reflecting pool surrounded by perfectly manicured, brightly colored flower beds.

Rollins slowed the limousine as he approached the double-doored entrance.

"Here we are!" Caitlin cried cheerfully as the car hummed to a halt. "Come inside." Caitlin led the way out of the Bentley. "Rollins will bring in the luggage." As she motioned the others through the doorway into the front foyer of the house, one of the maids was waiting there for them.

"Hi, Margaret," Caitlin addressed her. "How are you today?"

"Just fine, Miss Ryan."

"These are my friends, Emily Michaels, Jed Michaels, Diana Chasen."

"Pleased to meet you." The maid bobbed her head to the others. Caitlin noticed the three of them looking around at the impressive interior, taking in the beauty of the high-ceilinged hall with its crystal chandelier, the graceful, curving staircase, the priceless oil paintings on the walls, the Persian carpet on the gleaming marble floor, the Chippendale side chairs, and Hepplewhite hall table.

As Rollins came through the front entrance with the bags and set them to the side on the floor, a door opened at the far end of the hall, and Regina Ryan stepped out.

"Ah, Caitlin." Regina Ryan's smooth, cultured voice carried down the length of the hall. She continued speaking as she walked toward her granddaughter. "So good to see you. The rooms are all ready." As Caitlin met her at the edge of the hall, Mrs. Ryan offered a cheek for Caitlin's kiss.

"Hello, Grandmother," Caitlin said quietly, her manner more subdued than what it usually was at Highgate.

Mrs. Ryan's gaze swept over the three others.

"Grandmother," Caitlin put in quickly, "I'd like you to meet my friends." She motioned the others forward. "This is Emily Michaels. Her father owns Brookridge Farm. Emily, my grandmother, Mrs. Ryan."

"How do you do, Mrs. Ryan," Emily said politely, extending her hand.

Mrs. Ryan took Emily's fingers briefly, nodding her perfectly coiffed silver head. "I purchased a breeding mare from your father last autumn. He runs a fine establishment."

"Thank you." Emily blushed. "He'll be pleased to hear that."

"And this is Jed Michaels," Caitlin hurried on. "Emily's cousin. Jed recently came East from Montana and enrolled in Highgate this term."

Not the least unnerved by Mrs. Ryan's formality, Jed smiled easily and shook her hand, enveloping her small, white fingers in his long, tanned ones. "A pleasure to meet you, Mrs. Ryan."

"Montana, you say." Regina Ryan smiled slightly, charmed by Jed's easygoing ways. "And what brings you to Virginia?"

"My father wanted me to go to a good college-prep school. Since his brother lives nearby, we decided on Highgate."

"And how are you enjoying it?"

"I like it just fine." Jed's white teeth flashed in a grin. Caitlin noticed that his western drawl had deepened since he'd been talking to her grandmother. She sensed it was deliberate on his part, and it had precisely the right effect on Mrs. Ryan.

"I'm certainly no stranger to horses," he continued, "though the riding here is a little different from what I do at our cattle ranch."

Regina Ryan chuckled. "I would say. I tried my hand at riding a cattle pony once while visiting some friends in Texas. I'm afraid I wasn't very successful."

"There's a knack to it."

"Very good to meet you, Jed. I hope you'll have a pleasant time this weekend."

"Thank you, ma'am."

Regina Ryan had turned to the third of Caitlin's guests.

"And this is Diana Chasen, Grandmother. She's new to Highgate this year, too."

"Nice to meet you, Mrs. Ryan." Diana's voice was barely audible in her nervousness, but she gave the older woman a sweet, shy smile.

"Another newcomer." Mrs. Ryan arched her eyebrows. With one look of her steel blue eyes, she critically analyzed Diana's appearance and inexpensive attire. Caitlin could almost feel Diana shrinking into herself, but she did nothing to remedy her discomfort.

"We moved here from Norfolk this past summer.

My—my father's with the Department of Agriculture."

"Diana's on scholarship at Highgate," Caitlin added pleasantly, as though that bit of information would enhance Diana's image.

"I see," Regina Ryan said coolly, reacting exactly as Caitlin had known she would. "You must be an excellent student." She turned abruptly, cutting off Diana in the middle of her "Thank you, Mrs. Ryan." "Ginny is coming, I presume."

"She should be here in a little while, along with the others." The warmth her grandmother extended toward Ginny bothered Caitlin, but she didn't let it show.

"Very well. Margaret will show everyone to their rooms. I'll be having dinner with the Prestons but will be home before eleven." She turned briefly to the others and nodded to them. "Enjoy yourselves." She turned and set off down the hall toward her study.

When she was gone, Caitlin smiled at the others. "Well, let's get settled. Margaret, can you show Emily and Diana to their rooms? I can get my own bag," she added as the maid stooped to pick up the luggage.

"Let me take those from you." Jed whisked the bags from Margaret. "I'm bigger than you and need the exercise." He winked.

"You shouldn't—" she began, but Jed was already heading toward the stairs behind Emily and Diana, frustrating the plans Caitlin had for showing him to his room herself. She quickly followed behind up the curving staircase, her canvas shoulder bag suddenly an unwelcome weight. But as they started down the upstairs hall, Jed slowed his pace to walk beside her. He leaned over with a twinkle in his eyes and spoke quietly. "Your grandmother's quite a lady. After what you told me, I was wondering what she was like."

"Were you surprised?" she asked, giving him a sidelong gaze.

"Not a bit."

"I noticed you handled her pretty well."

"They teach us more than roping steers on the ranch," he teased.

Caitlin had the greatest urge to lift up a finger and touch the cleft in his strong chin, but even as she watched his laughing face, Jed suddenly grew serious. "I only wish I could have softened up her treatment of Diana."

"I was sorry about that," Caitlin lied with total lack of shame.

"There was nothing you could do. I could see your grandmother sizing Diana up and Diana falling to pieces."

"My grandmother can be very insensitive sometimes. I don't think she even realizes it."

They'd reached the turn in the hall that led to the bedrooms Emily and Diana would be using. The others paused at the corner.

"I'll show them to their rooms, Miss Ryan," the maid said brightly, thinking she was helping Caitlin out. "You go on ahead to your room and freshen up. I've laid out clean towels and things for you."

"Thank you, Margaret." Caitlin hid her dismay at having her conversation with Jed ended so abruptly, but it had been a very positive start, and she could soothe herself with that thought. "Let's all meet in the game room in about an hour or so," she told Emily and Diana.

"Great," Emily answered. "That'll give me time to get unpacked and soak in a tub. See you then."

Lastly Caitlin looked at Jed. Her lips were turned upward slightly in a tight smile that conveyed a silent message. "Your room's at the other end of the hall. Margaret will show you."

"Fine. I'll drop off the girls' bags and meet you all downstairs later."

She nodded with the same secret smile, then turned and started down the hall to her own room, sensing Jed was watching her.

As she stepped into the bedroom and closed the door behind her, she paused for a minute on the threshold. The entire room was done in blue and rose, her favorite colors. Two tall windows faced out toward the front lawns and were draped in blue brocade. On the wall opposite the door was a marble fireplace. Near it was a rose upholstered chaise longue with reading lamp. Along the wall across from the windows were matching twin canopy beds covered in old lace with bedspreads to match the curtains. Built-in bookcases filled one corner of the room, and a cherry-wood lady's secretary graced the other.

Beautiful as it was, Caitlin never had the same welcoming feeling here as she did at the dorm. The room she shared with Ginny seemed like home to her; this didn't.

She walked across the thick, dusty-rose carpet and dropped her canvas shoulder bag on one of the beds. First she'd take a long bubble bath, then she'd decide on exactly the right outfit to wear that night. It had to be special, because that night she was going to make her move.

10

An hour later, Caitlin was ready to put her weekend plans into action.

The noise level on the main floor had increased considerably with the arrival of the rest of her guests. Margaret had shown them into the game room that overlooked the swimming pool and formal backyard garden. Terry and Steve were engrossed in a game of pool near the back windows, Morgan and Dorothy were aiming darts at the board fastened to one of the walls, and a few others were lounging on the modular furniture grouped around the fireplace.

Caitlin sauntered into the room and up to Ginny, who was searching through the large record collection. After greeting her, Caitlin whispered, "Have you seen Jed?"

"Not yet," Ginny said, "though I haven't paid much attention because I've been going through the records. This place needs some music." She looked up at her roommate. "Boy, you're dressed to kill."

"Like it, huh?" Caitlin had opted for a shiny, black-leather pants set. Despite her grandmother's admonition about black being too dreary a color for her, Caitlin knew how sleek she looked in the tapered pants with matching body-tight jacket. Her long, flowing black hair added just the right casual touch so she wouldn't look out of place among her mostly jeans-clad friends.

"You'll have every guy in the room after you—as usual," Ginny sighed.

As if to prove her point, Roger approached the two girls. "So the hostess has finally decided to make an appearance. . . ."

As Roger began to tell her about the soccer team's latest exploits, Caitlin looked around the room. Jed was nowhere to be seen. Tim and Brett soon joined them, and by the time Caitlin found an opening in the conversation to politely excuse herself, Jed had arrived. And Diana was with him.

Damn, Caitlin muttered to herself. She'd wanted to get in a few words privately with him before they all sat down to dinner, but that would be impossible with *her* around. Caitlin's distress was only momentary, however, when she realized there'd still be time to corner Jed before the movie she'd planned for later that evening. Caitlin was confident she'd be the one sitting next to him at that point.

But after dinner, when everyone settled down around the projection TV to watch the movie, the feeling of success that Caitlin had had since her conversation with Jed that afternoon had dis-

appeared. Jed had taken a seat right next to Diana
on the couch. It was obvious that Diana must have
said something to Jed about her discomfort at Ryan
Acres, and he was playing the protector. Caitlin
barely watched the movie as she desperately tried
to think of some way to split the two of them up.

Finally, when the movie was over, Caitlin went
into action. Margaret and Rollins were passing out
sodas, and Roger had put on the stereo. As
Morgan, Tim, and Ginny searched through the
shelves of records and tapes, Brett Perkins and
Dorothy started to dance. A second later Gloria
and Roger joined them, but Jed and Diana didn't
budge from the couch. Caitlin walked over to them
and addressed Diana directly.

"Hi. I haven't had a chance to talk to you all
night, and I just realized you haven't met everyone, have you?"

"No, but that's okay. You've been busy, and Jed
and I have been talking." She glanced up at him
and gave him a sweet smile. She looked much
more relaxed than she had earlier in the afternoon.

Nothing could have fueled Caitlin's anger more
surely. Her eyes narrowed, but her voice held a
warm welcome as she laid a hand on Diana's
shoulder. "Let me introduce you now. Things will
be so hectic in the morning, and if you're thinking
of playing tennis with Jill and Steve, you should
meet them and make some plans tonight." She
stepped away, glancing back over her shoulder.
"Come on. They're right over there."

She left Diana no choice but to follow her

reluctantly, and while they were gone, Roger went over to talk to Jed. Caitlin knew perfectly well that Diana would have nothing in common with Jill and Steve, but she left the three of them talking and went back to Jed and Roger, settling herself casually in a chair opposite them. She began to question them about the soccer team's progress.

"Well, if you came out to practice more often, Caitlin," Roger chided, "you'd know exactly how we were doing."

"I know. I know." Caitlin laughed. "But I've been so busy with the fund-raiser and riding. I just don't have time for everything."

Just then Caitlin saw Diana look over in their direction. There was a worried, lost expression on her face. Emily, Diana's only other anchor, was totally absorbed in a conversation with Terry at the other side of the room and didn't even notice Diana's discomfort. *Good*, Caitlin thought, *let her sweat for a while. I've done more than my share.*

Caitlin succeeded in keeping Jed and Diana separated for the rest of the night, and when she ushered everyone out of the game room and upstairs, they had time only for a quick good night.

Caitlin had asked Ginny to share her own huge bedroom, and as the two girls walked down the hall after leaving the others, Ginny spoke in a conspiratorial voice.

"Okay, spitfire, what have you got planned now?"

"Why, nothing." Caitlin shrugged.

"That may work with some people, but not your

old buddy here." Ginny chuckled. "After watching you tonight, I have to say you've got a gift. I'm surprised Jed didn't see right through you."

"Really, Ginny, I don't know what you're talking about. All I tried to do was be a good hostess."

"Never mind. I can see I'm just going to have to wait to watch the drama unfold. Just remember that warning I gave you: Jed isn't playing with Diana. She's too nice a girl—and nice girls don't always finish last."

"Ginny, you can be so depressing sometimes. I wonder why I have you as a friend. By the way, why didn't you invite Bert?"

"Bert Simpson?" Ginny asked innocently.

Caitlin grinned. "You don't have to play coy with me. I've seen you two talking in the stables lately and put two and two together. You should have asked him to come."

"What, and have the whole group talking about me the way they do everyone else? Besides, I'm not ready yet. I told you, we're just friends. Anyway, I'd just as soon keep my private stuff private."

"That's up to you. Boy, am I tired!"

"Yeah, let's get to bed. Tomorrow's going to be another busy day."

The next morning, Caitlin wasted no time in pursuing her plans. After breakfast, as her guests rose from the table to mingle in groups around the dining room, Caitlin moved casually in Jed's direction. Luckily he and Roger had come down late for the meal, and since the only two empty seats were at the opposite end of the table from Diana, Jed and Diana hadn't had a chance to talk.

But now, as Caitlin started forward, she saw Diana head in Jed's direction as well. The expression on the girl's face was full of confusion and uncertainty. Caitlin paused a moment to decide how to counter Diana's latest move.

Unexpectedly Emily stopped at Caitlin's side. "I've been worried about Diana, Caitlin," she whispered. "She told me last night that she doesn't feel good enough about her tennis to play with Jill and Steve. She's afraid she'll make a fool of herself."

"Oh, that's too bad," Caitlin said with feigned concern, her eyes following Diana's progress across the room.

"I don't think she'd tell you she's unhappy. But do you think you could come up with something for her to do?"

"Sure. There are plenty of things to do around here by yourself." Caitlin spoke from experience, having spent so many lonely hours at the sprawling estate. "Don't worry a second more. I've got everything under control. Tell her to meet me in the game room. I'll be there in a minute."

It wasn't difficult, once Diana was safely out of the room, for Caitlin to casually sidle over to Jed. He was in riding clothes, but unlike the others, he wore jeans and a sweater rather than jodhpurs. The style suited him much better. He seemed thoughtful and looked up quickly when Caitlin spoke from behind his shoulder.

"I was just telling Emily about the horse I've got picked out for you. I think you're going to like him a lot."

Jed nodded distractedly and glanced over her shoulder to the hallway that led to the game room. He wasn't smiling. "Exactly who's riding?" he asked.

"Why, everyone, except Jill and Steve."

"And Diana?"

"Well, no. When I found out she didn't ride, I tried to get up a foursome for her at tennis. Now I just heard she doesn't play tennis, either. I feel badly about it—"

"Then I won't be riding, either," Jed announced.

Caitlin's eyes were wide with confusion. "I don't understand," she said. She felt thrown off guard and looked at him in alarm. "But I've given you the best horse in the stables—Challenger. You'll love him!"

"I'm sorry, Caitlin, but I don't want Diana to spend the day all by herself."

"No one said she had to. I was just going to talk to her, to make some suggestions."

The others had begun to drift out of the dining room. No one was listening to their conversation.

"Look, Caitlin, Diana's been uncomfortable from the time she got here."

"It's not my fault that she hasn't got any interests."

"I'm not saying it is. She has plenty of interests.

She just doesn't come from a family that could afford to give her riding and tennis lessons."

"Are you saying I shouldn't have invited her?" Caitlin's eyes were flashing in indignation.

"No. All I'm saying is that she feels left out."

"And I thought she'd feel left out if I *didn't* invite her. Jed, I hardly know her or what she likes and doesn't like, and it's hard enough keeping twelve other kids happy!"

For an instant Jed's expression softened, and Caitlin took full advantage of it. Her chin trembled, and as she blinked her eyes, her long lashes darkened with tears. "I'm doing the best I can. . . ."

"Caitlin, listen." Jed was uncomfortable. A slight flush darkened his cheekbones. "I don't mean to make you upset. I'm just worried about Diana."

"Well, so am I." She looked up at him hesitantly, her blue eyes luminous with tears. "I don't know what else to do but go ahead with the plans I've already made."

"Okay, I'm sorry." He sighed heavily. "Look, everyone's waiting."

"Then you'll come riding after all?" A note of hope was back in her voice.

He shook his head. "I'm going to find Diana. We'll see you at lunch." His words cut Caitlin to the core.

She wanted to scream, to lash out at him. He didn't care about her feelings, her disappointment. All he cared about was his sweet little Diana. She swallowed hard to keep her fury inside and nodded, afraid to say any more and reveal her real emotions. She refused even to look up at him as he patted her shoulder and walked quickly away.

Caitlin stood frozen to the spot for several seconds, seething as she listened to Jed's footsteps fading behind her. Her hands were clenched so tightly at her sides that her fingernails cut into her palms. This couldn't be happening to her! she thought. And all because of that prissy nothing of a girl! She'd get Diana back for this. She'd have her revenge if it was the last thing she did!

11

But hard as she tried, Caitlin could find no way of prying Jed from Diana's grasp. Unwilling to give him up but unable to win him over, Caitlin spent the next few weeks busy with the student council fund-raiser. During nearly all her free time she attended to the details of the show.

After a long day of work, Caitlin usually went back to the dorm and spent the hours before bedtime alone. She couldn't escape the painful images in her mind of Diana and Jed together. And Caitlin hadn't been able to rid herself of these thoughts by going out with other boys, either; her ploys to get them out of her hair had worked only too well. Terry and Emily were seeing each other constantly, as were Brett and Dorothy. Even Roger had become noticeably cooler toward her after the weekend at Ryan Acres, when he had begun dating Gloria.

The afternoon before the fund-raising show, the full committee and all the contestants gathered in the auditorium for a dress rehearsal. Caitlin was nearly beside herself, her clipboard overflowing with notes and last-minute reminders. But she was happy. The show was a sellout and would reap quite a sum for the scholarship fund. All around her, committee members were hurrying back and forth setting up the backdrop, the announcer's podium, and a set of risers for the contestants. Caitlin had arranged for the auditorium to be undisturbed during the next day. She'd also talked the headmaster, Dr. Foster, into presenting the awards. She herself would be the mistress of ceremonies.

As Morgan stood onstage behind Caitlin, calling directions to the four boys positioning the backdrop, Dorothy ran up with the latest article from one of the area newspapers. "They were only going to put in a little paragraph," she burst out excitedly, "until I mentioned your grandmother's name."

"I figured that would do the trick." Caitlin grinned. "If you see Brad Johnson, tell him to come see me. He's supposed to be working the lights, and we're going to be ready for him pretty soon." Caitlin's eyes scanned the group of kids gathered around the stage and on it. All of the committee members were present, with one glaring exception: Jed. Although the two of them had barely spoken since the weekend at Ryan Acres, Jed had lived up to his promise to help with the backstage crew. She couldn't believe he wouldn't show up for the dress rehearsal!

Caitlin was jarred from her thoughts as Gloria came running over. "Come help me! These guys are impossible. I'm trying to get them into their costumes, and they just *won't* cooperate. Tim keeps telling me his outfit makes him look like a jerk—and he's the one who decided to be Napoleon because his father had the costume up in their attic!"

"That's easy. I'll just go over and tell him how gorgeous he looks."

"But that's not all. Roger's decided he doesn't want to be Superman now, and Jerry Davis, who said he'd get his whole costume together himself, came with nothing but jeans and a plaid shirt. What kind of costume do you call that?"

"Okay, Gloria. I'll talk to them."

Caitlin walked to the side of the stage where the boys were gathered. Within minutes she had Tim believing he'd never looked handsomer than he did in his high-collared white shirt and long-tailed jacket. She also thanked him profusely for being the only one with the class to come in a historical costume. Roger, too, was soon pacified when Caitlin stood back and studied him.

"Wow, Roger, you can really see how athletic you are when you wear that outfit. It looks like you lift weights."

"I do," he said proudly.

"Then why are you worried about the Superman costume? The judges will love it!" Then she whispered, "And I think it looks sexy."

He blushed, then shrugged. "Yeah, I guess I was being stupid."

But Jerry Davis wasn't so easy. He stood stubbornly with his hands at his sides.

"Maybe I'm a little dense," Caitlin said, "but what are you supposed to be?"

"A farmer."

"Oh, sure," said Caitlin. "I don't know why I didn't realize that. But I think you'd look even better if you had a few props . . . you know, like a straw hat and maybe a pitchfork."

"I don't have any of that stuff." Jerry had been coerced by some of his friends into being a contestant, and he wanted everyone to know it.

"I can get you a straw hat," Gloria volunteered. "I have one at the dorm. But a pitchfork?"

"There's bound to be one on campus somewhere," Caitlin said. "Maybe in the stables. Why don't you go take a look, Jerry?"

"No, no, he can't go anywhere!" Gloria interrupted. "Jessica's almost ready to start them through the introductory number. If I let even one of the guys out of my sight, she'll kill me."

"Yeah, understandable." Caitlin nodded. She herself had ordered the guys to run through every step of the script she and Jessica had written. "And Pete's ready with the music. He has to leave at six for a tutoring session."

Caitlin had grown thoughtful as Gloria had been speaking. Jed still hadn't appeared, and she suspected that he was at the Fosters' keeping Diana company while she baby-sat. It infuriated her that he'd rather be with Diana than at her rehearsal.

But her anger gave way to inspiration when she remembered that the groundskeeper's maintenance shed was in back of the faculty house occupied by the Fosters. She knew there was a pitchfork inside it.

114

They could do without her at the rehearsal for ten minutes, she rationalized to herself. In the process she'd accomplish two missions. She'd get the pitchfork, *and* she'd be able to find out if Jed actually was with Diana!

"Don't worry about it, Gloria," Caitlin said breezily. "I'll get someone to run over."

Caitlin walked back across the stage and looked around to make sure that everything was under control for the moment. Then she dropped her clipboard on the front of the stage and jumped down the steps to the auditorium floor. No one even noticed her going out the side door. If she hurried, she thought, she could be across the lawns to the faculty housing in two minutes.

She ran the distance over the back lawns to the three brick houses occupied by the heads of Highgate. As headmaster, Dr. Foster and his wife had the largest house on the end with its own yard, which ran along the side and in back of the house. In one corner of the fenced-in yard was the school maintenance shed. Caitlin had been in the shed before, getting tools to plant the window boxes she and Ginny had hung outside their dorm windows the previous spring, so she knew that a pitchfork was stored there. She figured the groundskeeper wouldn't mind having the student council borrow it.

Her eyes were focused more on the headmaster's house than on the shed as she unlatched the gate and made her way across the yard. The Fosters' six-year-old son, Ian, was playing with his trucks in a sandbox at the far corner of the yard and didn't notice her. Caitlin strained to look inside the windows, hoping to see Jed, but she couldn't see anyone. Angrily she muttered under her breath. Had she made this trip for nothing?

She reached for the doorknob, turned it, and tugged. It didn't budge. She tugged again in frustration. It was locked. Looking above the doorsill, she saw the key hanging from a nail and took it down. She glanced back over her shoulder just as Diana appeared at the back door. Not wanting Diana to see her, Caitlin ducked around the side of the shed. She heard Diana's quiet but stern voice. "Ian, I'll be back in a second. There's someone at the front door."

Caitlin peeked around the corner and saw Diana retreating into the dark house. *It must be Jed,* she thought angrily.

Quickly Caitlin put the key into the lock and turned it. After sticking the key back up on the nail, she swung the door open with a bang. Once inside the shed, she went to the corner where the tools were kept. The newer ones were hanging on the wall, while the older tools were leaning in a heap in the corner. She began rummaging through the maze of wooden handles searching for the pitchfork.

Longing to be outside and spying on the activity in the house, Caitlin cast the long handles aside impatiently. Several fell and jammed against a shelf. She dislodged them with a forceful push, and they rattled to the floor, taking with them some of the contents of the shelf—some plastic containers and filled paper sacks. "Damn!" Caitlin muttered angrily, quickly picking up a couple of them and throwing them on the shelf. She left the others and went back to trying to find the pitchfork.

At last she found it. After disentangling it, she dragged it out to the middle of the floor and pushed the rest of the unwanted tools back up against the wall. Her hair was falling in her eyes in a tangled mess. Brushing it away from her cheek with a dust-covered hand, she picked up the pitchfork and headed toward the door.

She stepped out of the shed, kicked the door shut, and started slowly across the yard. Ian Foster still hadn't noticed her. Again Caitlin tried to peer through the windows of the house, but she couldn't see or hear anything.

As she neared the gate, she thought she heard the front door of the house open and close. Just then the phone began to ring inside the house. Caitlin hurried forward; she had to see if Jed might be leaving the house. Maybe he'd just dropped by on his way to the rehearsal. But the latch on the gate was stuck, and it took her a few moments to get it open. By the time she rounded the corner of the house and had a clear view of the front door, no one was in sight. Shaking her head in frustration, she started back toward the auditorium with the pitchfork. She entered through the backstage door and paused in the wings, watching the commotion onstage.

Jessica was standing in front and had just started

the boys through their initial parade onstage. "No, Tim, a little to the left—you're blocking Jim," she cried out. "Jerry, do you have to look so miserable?"

"Yeah, because I am!" he called back.

Caitlin stepped out of the wings. "Well, Jerry," she called, "we've managed to find one prop for your costume." Smiling, she handed him the pitchfork. "If these other guys get in the way, you can always give them a poke."

He took the handle in his hand. "A poke? Hey, with this thing, I could send them right off the stage."

"Now, just wait a second," Roger yelled.

"Your hat will be here tomorrow, Jerry," Caitlin added smoothly. "Now how about getting back to rehearsal. All joking around aside, you guys know how important this fund-raiser is."

Caitlin stepped down from the stage and, keeping a constant eye on what was going on, walked up one of the aisles toward the back. Ginny was seated in the last row, her paperwork spread all around her. Dorothy was leaning against the wall behind her, reading Ginny's figures.

"How's it going?" Caitlin asked.

Ginny looked up. "If we sell out the standing room tickets, we'll make about three thousand dollars."

"Fantastic!" Caitlin exclaimed. Her grandmother would be delighted to hear that. "I hope we sell them."

"How can we not?" Ginny countered. "The whole county's talking about this show. Your contest idea was pure inspiration."

"I'm glad you've finally seen the light." Caitlin winked.

Back on the stage, Jessica was directing the boys to their places and not having an easy time of it. Caitlin could see she needed help and started down the aisle. She jumped up onto the stage and took the laser sword from Matt Jenks's Darth Vader costume.

"Okay, you guys," she announced, brandishing the prop as she walked in front of them. "We've got a show to put on here. People are actually paying money to see you. Are you really going to make them leave here disappointed tomorrow night? Or are you going to show them what you're really made of?" She threw the laser back at Matt, who fumbled a little before catching it.

Roger spoke up. "Caitlin's right, boys. We can't let the audience down."

As if on cue, Pete, the music director, restarted the music. Caitlin's brief speech had had its desired effect. Suddenly the boys began to do exactly what they were supposed to. They ran through their opening group number, laughing, joking, making a true production of it. Caitlin couldn't believe how good they were. The audience would be rolling in the aisles.

Meanwhile, she watched as Roger strode across the stage, his Superman cape flaring behind him. Jerry sauntered with his new pitchfork, and Tim walked proudly in his Napoleon costume. As Bill Ferrari, the last of the twelve contestants, finished his parade around the stage, a late entry and a surprise to everyone stepped out from backstage.

Caitlin

"Oh, my God, I don't believe it," Dorothy gasped. "A princess. What a costume. Who is it? Or should I say, 'what is it'?"

"I'm not sure." Caitlin could barely believe her eyes herself. No one had told her there was another contestant signed up. "But it looks like Laurence Baxter. It's kind of hard to tell with all that makeup he's got on."

"Impossible!" Dorothy was shaking her head. "Laurence? Dressed like that? He's too serious. All he ever thinks about is studying."

"I know." Caitlin nodded.

"Just because he's a brain, doesn't mean he can't have fun," Ginny shot in.

"But why did he sign up for this? He's never been to any of the meetings."

"Maybe Diana talked him into it," Ginny mused. "They're good friends."

"Her?" Caitlin said with disgust. "She never even ended up joining a committee!"

"She's busy."

"Busy? I think she just wants everyone to feel sorry for her. Anyway, we've got another contestant."

"He'll get first place."

"Maybe." Suddenly Caitlin lifted her head. "What's that noise?"

"What noise?" Ginny asked.

"Can't you hear it? Almost like a siren."

"If there were a fire, we'd all know about it. The school alarm would be going off."

"Yeah," Dorothy added. "It's probably a fire truck going to rescue a cat out of a tree."

120

But several of the crew members had begun to cluster by the rear backstage door, which had been swung open. Roger and Tim disappeared out the door.

"It's an ambulance," someone cried out, "over by the faculty houses."

"Really?" Caitlin pushed through the crowd. It was almost impossible to see anything with the trees blocking the view across the lawns. "Is someone sick?"

"We don't know. Roger and Tim went over to check."

Caitlin turned from the door. She had to regain control; there was still over half a show to rehearse.

"Okay, guys," she said authoritatively, "somebody will let us know what happened. It's probably nothing. Meantime, everybody onstage again!" With Caitlin leading the way, the others filed unenthusiastically away from the door. Caitlin had gone partway through her checklist when Tim came running in from outside.

"It's the Foster kid," he shouted. "They've taken him to the hospital!"

Unconsciously Caitlin clenched her clipboard. She'd just seen Ian Foster. "What happened?"

Tim shook his head. "We couldn't get close enough to see, and nobody would tell us anything. The paramedics were working on him, and then they took him off in the ambulance."

"Diana Chasen baby-sits for him," someone murmured.

Tim nodded. "Yeah. I saw her get in the ambulance. She seemed really shook."

"Where were the Fosters?"

"I heard someone say they'd gone out of town for a meeting or something and would be back late."

"I hope it's nothing serious." Caitlin tried to keep her voice steady. She felt vaguely uneasy, almost as if her having just seen Ian made her responsible somehow for the boy's condition.

The rest of the kids seemed pretty stunned, too. "We might as well call it quits for today," Caitlin said finally. "Get here two hours earlier than we planned tomorrow."

12

"Diana, I just spoke to one of the doctors."

Diana Chasen, pale and trembling, looked up into the strong but kindly face of Lorin Michaels, Emily Michaels's father. Diana's own parents were away in Pennsylvania with her dying grandmother.

"Yes?" Diana's voice quavered. She'd been sitting on the same hard bench in the hospital for four hours, waiting, numb, torn apart with anguish.

"Although Ian appears to be suffering from a concussion, there are also traces of poison in his system. They believe it's one of the chemicals from the sacks in the shed."

"No—oh, no!" The words were torn from her in a harsh cry. She covered her face with her hands and seemed to shrink into a ball. "That's impossible! I locked the shed door. I know it!"

"But it was unlocked when you found him on the back steps." Mr. Michaels sat beside her and laid a hand gently on her shoulder. "I don't want to make this any more difficult for you than it already is. We all know how upset you are."

"I just want you to believe me!"

"I do. But we all make mistakes. Perhaps you were in a hurry. Perhaps the lock didn't catch—"

"But if that door was unlocked, then it's my fault! I was so careful. Really, Mr. Michaels, I was!"

"Diana—"

But the girl rushed on through broken sobs. "Mrs. Foster told me before she left for work that some delivery men were coming—that I was to be sure the shed was locked after they left. And I *was* sure. I remember hanging up the key!"

Just then a white-frocked doctor stepped out of Ian Foster's room at the far side of the corridor. Mr. Michaels rushed up to him.

"How is he doing?"

"Right now he's stable, though comatose. We've given him an antidote. Considering his age and general good health, I think his chances for recovery are quite good. But I can make no promises at this point. We won't know for sure until he comes out of the coma." The weary doctor took off his glasses and rubbed his eyes. "He never should have been allowed near that stuff."

"Diana says she's positive she locked that shed door," Mr. Michaels said. "Is there any chance Ian's accident was caused by something else?"

The doctor shook his head sadly. "I've talked to the paramedics who were at the scene. The boy was lying on the back stairs of the house. The shed door was wide open. When they went in, they found two open sacks of the chemical on the floor.

They brought a sample with them. We have to assume the boy went inside to explore, ate enough of the poison to make himself ill, then went back outside and tried to get into the house. That's when he fell and injured his head. It's unusual for a six-year-old to sample an unknown substance. But unfortunately, the chemical looked remarkably like powdered sugar."

"I see. Do the Fosters know this?"

The doctor nodded. "I suggest you keep the girl away from them. Take her home, but don't let her be alone." He wagged his head. "They'll calm down eventually. It's their anxiety—I've seen it happen before."

Mr. Michaels sighed. "I'll take her back to my place. My daughter and nephew are there." He extended his hand. "Thank you."

After the doctor left, Mr. Michaels returned to Diana. "I'm going to take you home now. You can stay with us until your parents arrive."

Diana sat frozen in the seat. "I can't leave him. You must know that, Mr. Michaels. I'm responsible for him."

"Diana, there's nothing more you can do here. You need some rest."

"No." Diana was gazing at him with wide eyes. "I have to stay. The Fosters would be upset."

Lorin Michaels recognized the signs of shock. Firmly he leaned down to place an arm about her waist and lifted her from the seat. "The Fosters are here," he lied. "They're with Ian right now. They want you to go home and rest. Come along now. The car's right outside. Emily and Jed are waiting."

"The Fosters are here? You're sure he'll be all right?"

"Yes, I'm sure."

Only then did Diana allow him to lead her from the room.

As they stepped through the front door of the Michaels home, Emily and Jed rushed out from the living room to meet them.

"Dad, Diana, I'm so glad you're here!" The worry on Emily's face was evident as she looked back and forth between her father and the white-faced Diana.

"Let me take Diana into the living room." Jed's tone was gentle as he stepped forward to place an arm around Diana's shoulders. "You'll feel better," he added quietly to her, "when you sit down and relax. Have you eaten?"

"I don't remember. Did we, Mr. Michaels?" She turned to look back at him.

"No, as a matter of fact, we haven't, and that's an excellent idea."

"I have the dinner leftovers already warming." Ellen Michaels came hurrying down the hall to put an arm around her husband and kiss him on the cheek. "We've been so worried. How is he?"

"We'll talk about it later." He sighed wearily. "Diana's been through enough."

"No good?" his wife whispered.

"No."

Jed had already taken Diana into the living

room, but Emily was still standing in the hall and heard her parents' words.

"What's wrong, Dad?" Emily was close to tears herself. "Why is Diana acting so strangely? It frightens me."

"She's in shock, sweetheart. She needs time and rest." He swallowed. "Ian Foster is suffering from both poisoning and a concussion. Somehow he got into a shed that was supposed to be locked—"

"Oh, my God!"

"Shhh." Lorin Michaels silenced his daughter. "We'll talk about this later. Don't let Diana see you so upset. It'll only disturb her more."

When Mr. Michaels stepped into the living room, Jed looked up, a troubled expression on his face, but he said nothing. He'd settled Diana beside him on the couch and was sitting with his arm around her. Her head was resting on his shoulder, and her eyes were closed.

"I'm glad to see she's sleeping," Mr. Michaels said quietly.

Jed nodded as he glanced down at the girl at his side. Every so often Diana gave a deep sigh and shuddered. He was glad she was resting, too. She'd been through so much that day, and he instinctively knew that she'd need all the strength she could muster in the days to come.

13

As Caitlin and Ginny left the dorm for the dining room the next morning, Morgan, Dorothy, and Gloria joined them.

"Have you heard anything more about the Foster boy?" Dorothy asked.

"I tried to talk to Emily last night," Caitlin said, "but her father wouldn't let her come to the phone. He did tell me that Jed's there, too—and Diana."

"You're kidding?" Gloria stared. "It must be serious."

Caitlin nodded. She was the only one who knew that Diana hadn't been keeping a close eye on Ian, but she'd decided to keep that knowledge to herself for a while. Since Jed had probably been with her, Caitlin couldn't take the risk of implicating him in whatever had happened. "All I know is that Emily left a message with her roommate that Ian was in a coma."

"Oh, my God. From what?"

"They think he fell down and hit his head."

"I'm sure glad I'm not in Diana's shoes," Ginny said with more sympathy than the others had shown.

"She's got Emily and Jed there to hold her hand," Caitlin couldn't resist remarking.

Ginny frowned. "Do you hate her that much?"

"Who said anything about hating her? I wouldn't waste the energy." Caitlin wanted to add that if Ginny knew the truth, she wouldn't be feeling so sorry for Diana. But she bit back the words. She had to think about Jed.

"What's going to happen to the fund-raiser tonight?" Morgan asked. "Will we have to cancel it?"

"Cancel it?" Caitlin's eyes widened. "After all the work we've done? No way! Maybe we'll have to postpone it for a week. I'll check with the office. In fact, I think I'll do that right now. Hold a seat for me."

As the others headed for the dining room, Caitlin turned toward the administrative office. Mrs. Forbes was already at her desk, looking very worried.

"Mrs. Forbes," Caitlin asked quietly, "how's Ian?"

The older woman shook her head. "Still in a coma."

"Everyone was so upset to hear about it. What actually happened?"

"I don't know exactly, Caitlin. Dr. Foster was too upset to go into detail."

"What a shame. You know that the student

council fund-raiser is tonight. I was wondering if we should postpone it."

"No, no. One thing Dr. Foster did make clear was that everything should continue at Highgate as if nothing had happened."

Caitlin nodded. "Okay. I'll tell the rest of the committee."

As Caitlin walked away, she smiled to herself. She hadn't wanted to postpone the fund-raiser, and she was sure Jed would be back at the school by that night. She'd asked her grandmother to come, too, and couldn't wait to see her proud expression when she saw Caitlin emceeing. Regina Ryan would be so proud of that accomplishment!

"Good evening, ladies and gentlemen, and welcome to our show." Caitlin stood in the center of the auditorium stage dressed in a formal black tuxedo. "We've got something special planned for you tonight, the first-ever Highgate male beauty contest. Now, without further ado, let's introduce our contestants. Ready, Pete?"

Caitlin signaled to her music director to start up the first production number. All thirteen contestants marched onto the stage. The audience responded enthusiastically, the older members clapping politely while the Highgate students responded wildly with wolf calls and jeers. The loudest laughs were for Laurence Baxter's princess outfit. The junior boy had put on even more makeup than at the dress rehearsal. Dressed in a long, flowing gown and wearing a teased blond wig, the broad-shouldered boy teetered precariously on black patent leather heels.

While the boys took the stage, Caitlin walked off into the wings. "They're loving it!" Morgan exclaimed.

"Yes, they are," Caitlin said absently, distracted from the events onstage. Although it had admittedly been hard to see into the audience from the stage, she had managed to pick out a few familiar faces: Mr. Lowery from the union, her English teacher, Mr. Samuelson, and Roger Wake's parents.

But there was no sign of either Jed or her grandmother out there. She tried to console herself by thinking they were late and would be arriving soon, but in her heart she was forced to admit the truth—that neither one of them was likely to show up at all.

She went back onstage to introduce and to interview each contestant individually, then to introduce the judges. Caitlin knew her grandmother would have been impressed with the professional way she handled the proceedings. And Jed would have gotten a kick out of the way she deftly led the contestants through the hysterical question-and-answer part of the program. But, throughout the evening, every time Caitlin got another chance to peer into the crowd, her worst fears were confirmed. Still no Jed. No Regina Ryan. Caitlin hid her dismay behind a bright smile. No one, she vowed, would know how much she was hurting.

At the end of the evening, in Dr. Foster's absence, Caitlin presented the winners.

"Now for the third runner-up," she called, reaching for the first bouquet of plastic daisies. "Tim Collins . . . as Napoleon!"

A blushing Tim came forward to a roar of applause and took his position on the risers.

"Second runner-up . . . Matt Jenks as Darth Vader!"

More cheers and applause.

"First runner-up . . . Roger Wake as Superman."

The audience, the rest of the soccer team in particular, went wild. Roger was laughing as he picked up his bouquet.

"And now our fund-raiser beauty king . . . Princess Laurence Baxter!"

Laurence was grinning as he came forward and shook Caitlin's hand. She'd never had a chance to get to know Laurence very well, but she liked his smile, and she liked the firm grip of his handshake. Too bad he was such a good friend of Diana, she thought.

"Congratulations, Laurence! You deserve it." She lifted the foot-high tinsel crown and placed it on his oversized wig. He reached up to steady it.

When the applause in the audience had quieted down a bit, Caitlin went back to the mike. "Guys, thank you all for being such good sports! You were great. Before everyone leaves, I want to tell you that this year's fund-raiser has been an incredible success. So far it looks like we've made nearly three thousand dollars. Thanks for coming!" With that she blew the audience and contestants a kiss and stepped offstage.

But instead of hanging around to party with the rest of the kids, Caitlin gave each of the winners a hug and went back to her dorm. Despite the night's triumph, she felt she had little to celebrate.

"What a show!" Ginny cried, when she returned to the room a couple of hours later. She was still glowing from excitement over the night's activities. "You were great."

"Thanks," Caitlin said tiredly.

"How come you didn't go to the party? I thought you'd want to take your bows."

"I was beat. Besides, no one really cares about stuff like that." Quickly, before Ginny had a chance to question her, she asked, "Any more news about Ian Foster?"

Ginny shook her head. "Nothing that I've heard."

"When I didn't see Jed and Emily tonight, I wondered."

"How'd your grandmother like the show? Did she tell you?"

"She didn't come." Caitlin forced a lightness to her tone. "Something must have come up at the last minute—she always has these unexpected meetings and stuff, even on weekends."

"That's too bad." Ginny studied her roommate's face. "You must be disappointed."

Caitlin shook her head vigorously. "I know she would have been here if she could. Besides, my birthday's coming up next weekend. I know she'll make a big production out of it"—she was staring blindly down at the floor—"to make up for tonight."

That night Caitlin was thankful that Ginny was such a sound sleeper. While her roommate dozed blissfully, the most popular junior at Highgate Academy cried her heart out. She'd never felt sadder or lonelier in her life.

14

For two days everyone waited for news about Ian Foster. He remained in a coma, and with each passing hour Diana grew more depressed. She'd blocked out the details of the accident. All she remembered was that Ian was very sick.

She wandered about the Michaelses' house like a lost child until finally Jed went to his uncle. "We've got to do something for her," he pleaded. "I can't stand to see her this way."

"I don't know what to tell you. I asked the doctor at the hospital, and he said the shock would gradually pass. We just have to be patient with her."

"If only her parents would get here."

"They said they would be here as soon as they made the funeral arrangements for Diana's grandmother. I hope they'll be here tonight."

Just then the phone rang. A second later Ellen Michaels called from the kitchen extension. "Lorin, it's for you—the hospital."

Mr. Michaels and Jed exchanged nervous looks.

"Let's hope it's good news," Mr. Michaels said as he hurried to the phone with Jed on his heels.

Mrs. Michaels and Jed were waiting impatiently as Mr. Michaels hung up the phone. "The boy's regaining consciousness," he said. "It looks as if he'll have a full recovery! The doctor wanted Diana to know."

"Thank goodness!" Mrs. Michaels said, and sighed in relief. "Let me go tell the girls. They're up in Emily's room."

"I hope this makes a difference for her," Jed said.

A few moments later Diana came flying into the room, Emily on her heels. "Take me to the hospital. Please, I have to see Ian."

"Diana," Mr. Michaels said cautiously, "do you think that's a good idea? His parents are there with him."

"I have to see him! I have to know he's all right." Tears welled up in her eyes. "Please?"

Thirty minutes later, as Jed and Emily remained behind in the waiting room, Mr. Michaels took Diana to Ian's floor. He didn't intend to let the girl get as far as Ian's room, but to have her wait while he summoned the doctor. He paused at the nurses' station.

"I'm Lorin Michaels. I'd like to see the doctor in charge of Ian Foster's case."

The nurse on duty glanced up from the chart in her hands. "Oh, yes, Ian Foster. Room three twenty-four."

At her words, Diana shot off toward the room.

"Diana, wait!" Mr. Michaels cried. But it was too late. The girl had already stepped into the room.

The Fosters were seated to either side of their son's head, holding his hands. They looked haggard from their two-day vigil, but the moment they saw Diana their expressions turned to shock.

It was their son who broke the uncomfortable silence. "Diana," he called.

The nurse who was standing at the side of the room stepped forward. "He's only just regained consciousness. He shouldn't be disturbed."

But Diana paid no attention to her. Her face alight, she cried out. "Oh, Ian, Ian. I'm so glad to see you!" She started toward the bed.

As a delighted smile spread across his face, Ian started to sit up. His parents were too surprised to try to stop him. He was halfway into a sitting position when he suddenly fell back against the pillow.

"Ian, what's wrong?" his mother cried.

"Mommy, my legs are stuck. They don't work."

"What?" Richard Foster stared down at his son, then turned to the nurse. "Get Dr. Brower."

"I'm already here." The doctor, summoned by the nurse, hurried into the room. "What seems to be wrong?"

"It's his legs!" Elaine Foster burst out.

"Why don't we take a look at them?" The doctor smiled and drew back the sheet. Ian's sturdy little legs were stretched out on the bed. "Let's bend this leg up," Dr. Brower said, gently gripping Ian's right foot. "Go ahead, bend your knee."

Ian's face was a picture of frustration. "I can't! It won't move!"

"All right, don't get upset. Let's try the other one."

The procedure was repeated with the same lack of success.

"My son's paralyzed!" Mrs. Foster screamed.

"Mrs. Foster," Dr. Brower warned, casting a meaningful look at Ian, "there's no need to become so alarmed. If everyone would leave the room, I'd like to do some further tests."

"I'm not leaving my son! Not for a moment!" Mrs. Foster was close to tears. Dr. Brower nodded his consent, then continued with his examination.

Lorin Michaels drew a disbelieving Diana out into the hall.

Twenty minutes later the Fosters came out of the room. Mrs. Foster's head was buried against her husband's shoulder, and she was sobbing. Before Mr. Michaels could lay a restraining hand on Diana's arm, she rushed forward.

"Mrs. Foster, I have to tell you how sorry I am. I didn't leave that shed unlocked. I didn't!"

Elaine Foster swung around to face the girl. "You! You have the nerve to come here and tell me you're sorry! *Sorry?* What good does that do? Ian's crippled! He'll never walk again!"

Lorin had rushed up to put an arm around Diana. "Don't you think the girl is suffering—" he began.

But Ian's mother cut him off. "It's all her fault, all because of her carelessness!"

"Elaine, please." Dr. Foster tried to soothe her. "This won't help. It was an accident."

"I'll never forgive you!" she screamed at Diana. "You've crippled my child!"

"No! No!" Diana had utterly crumpled in Lorin Michaels's arms. Her words came out in broken sobs. "I didn't hurt him. I love Ian. I wouldn't . . ."

Mr. Michaels waited no longer. He took Diana by her shoulders and sped her down the hall.

By the time they were driving out of the hospital parking lot, the sedative the doctor had given Diana had taken effect, and she had fallen into an exhausted sleep. Mr. Michaels filled Emily and Jed in on Ian's condition and the terrible scene that had taken place.

"How could Mrs. Foster do that?" Emily cried.

"She was hysterical. People do strange things when they're stricken with grief."

Jed was silent. He only continued rubbing a soothing hand over Diana's shoulder.

When they reached the house, Mr. Michaels quickly ran inside to tell his wife what had happened. "Let's take her into the library," Mrs. Michaels instructed as Jed carried the sleeping Diana into the house. "We can leave the door open, and the couch in there is comfortable."

Mr. Michaels led the way into the library and turned on a dim lamp as Jed carefully laid Diana on the couch. She stirred as he withdrew his arms, and he leaned over to place a tender kiss on her brow.

"I'll sit with her for a while," Emily offered.

"That's not necessary, dear," her mother said softly.

"I want to. I feel like I have to do something."

"Geez," Jed moaned when they were back in the living room. "Why Diana? Why did something like this have to happen to her?"

"I realize how much you care about her, Jed, but I don't have any answers."

"No, I know you don't." Jed sighed and dropped his head into his hands. "What happens now?"

"I couldn't say exactly. One thing's certain. She should stay away from the Fosters—and Highgate—for the time being."

"She's in no condition to go back, anyway," Jed said wearily. "God, I'm scared for her."

"I think she'll be better after a good night's sleep. It's been too much for her."

"You remember how my sister was after our mother left?" Jed asked.

Mr. Michaels nodded. "You were good for her."

"Yeah, I suppose, but Annie wasn't anywhere near as bad as Diana."

"We'll just have to wait and see, Jed—"

The doorbell suddenly shrilled, making both men jump.

"I'll get it," Mrs. Michaels called from the hall.

From the sound of the voices in the hall, Jed could tell that the Chasens had arrived. Mrs. Michaels brought them into the living room. "This is my husband, Lorin. Lorin, Bud and Myrna Chasen. Perhaps it would be best if he talked to you. He was at the hospital. Your daughter's asleep in the library if you'd like to see her."

"We'd like to hear what your husband has to say first." Diana's mother spoke with a decided southern drawl, but her curt tone hardened her words. She was of medium height with black hair and slanting dark eyes; she might have been beautiful if not for the brittleness of her appearance—makeup a trifle too heavy, clothing a bit too flashy. It was obvious Diana took after her tall, sandy-haired father.

"I can't thank you enough for taking care of Diana," Mr. Chasen said. "She's all right?"

"As well as can be expected, I guess. She's resting for the moment. It's been quite a shock for her."

"Our conversation on the phone left so many questions in my mind. My daughter has always been so careful with children," Mr. Chasen said.

"It's all been pretty harrowing. Come, sit down. Can we get you coffee, something to eat?"

"I sure wouldn't mind a cup of coffee," his wife put in.

Ellen Michaels excused herself to get the coffee, and Mrs. Chasen turned to Lorin Michaels. "I can't remember such a week. First, Bud's mother, and then Diana getting herself in such a mess."

"She's not respons—" Jed began, but his uncle silenced him and began to tell the Chasens all the details of the unlocked shed and the poison the child had swallowed.

"No!" Mrs. Chasen had risen from her chair. "I won't hear such accusations against my daughter!"

"It was an accident, Mrs. Chasen," Mr. Michaels quickly put in. "No one is accusing Diana. Good heavens!"

"Well, someone's accusing her."

"Myrna, please—"

"No, Bud, I won't be still. We talked about this before. I told you no good could come from putting her in this hoity-toity school, but you wouldn't listen. No, no, Diana's got to have the best—and now look what's come of it."

Bud Chasen rose and took his wife's arm. "Myrna, I think we've imposed on the Michaelses' hospitality long enough." He looked at Lorin Michaels apologetically. "If you could show us where our daughter is?"

Mrs. Michaels had come into the room, a tray containing coffee cups, cream, and sugar in her hands. Quickly, she set it down and said, "Of course. Right this way."

As Mrs. Michaels led the Chasens to the library, Jed, his expression livid, came up behind his uncle. "You can't let them take her! My God, she's in bad enough shape already. That woman will totally drive her off the deep end."

"I know," his uncle said tiredly. "But there's nothing I can do, Jed. These are her parents. They have every right to take her."

"But we can't just let her go." Jed shook his head. "I don't like it, Uncle Lorin. I don't like it at all."

Ten minutes later the Chasens left the house, Diana wrapped in a blanket and asleep in her father's arms. Jed wanted to go to her, but Mrs. Chasen hovered around her husband and daughter, and no one else could get close.

"Tell her I'll call her tomorrow," Jed called out, "and that we're thinking of her."

But Mrs. Chasen ignored him, and Mr. Chasen's expression as he looked down at his daughter's face was so distraught that it was doubtful he even heard Jed's words.

"Her books and things are still at school," Emily cried, on the verge of tears. "I'll bring them to her so she can keep up with her work."

"There's no need for that," her mother snapped. "The school can send us her clothes. As for her books, she won't be needing them. I've no intention of letting her set foot in that school again."

15

"Caitlin! Caitlin! Have I got something to tell you!" Tenny Sears caught up to Caitlin on the brick path between the classroom buildings. The petite freshman was red faced from running and was panting heavily.

"What is it, Tenny?" Caitlin sounded distant, but she turned to face the girl.

"It's about Laurence. I heard he was so caught up by winning the contest that last night he paraded around the boys' dorm in his dress!"

The sparkle in Tenny's eyes faded quickly in light of the sharp glance Caitlin gave her. "You don't really expect me to believe that," Caitlin said. "Only a fool would believe it."

"Well, it sounded like the truth to me," Tenny said, looking embarrassed. Caitlin had begun to walk away, and Tenny had to take a few quick steps to catch up. "I'm going to the science building. Mind if I walk with you?"

"No, come along," Caitlin said. Just a few weeks ago she would have come up with some kind of excuse to avoid having Tenny follow her around, but right now she couldn't care less who she was seen with. It was four days after the fund-raiser, and she still hadn't heard a word from her grandmother. It depressed her that her grandmother could be so uncaring that she hadn't even asked how the fund-raiser had gone; after all, the proceeds *were* going to her favorite charity. But Caitlin also longed for some acknowledgment of her own performance that night. She'd worked so long and hard to make the evening a success. She didn't think it was too much to ask for some praise or at least some recognition from her grandmother.

There was something else bothering Caitlin, something she tried so hard to get out of her mind, yet couldn't: Ian Foster. The whole school had been buzzing with rumors about the accident, but no one was sure what really had happened, other than that the boy had received some kind of head injury. Caitlin didn't know how severe it was, but the latest rumor she'd heard was that Ian was being kept alive on a respirator. She didn't know whether or not this was true, but still Caitlin had a funny feeling about the accident. She had seen Ian such a short time before his fall that she couldn't help wondering if somehow she could have prevented the accident.

Caitlin spoke up again and almost absently asked Tenny, "Have you heard anything new about Ian Foster?"

Tenny frowned. "No." Then, a few moments later she pointed to their left. "But there's someone who might know."

Caitlin peered in the direction of the large willow that graced the south side of the science building.

Jed was sitting beneath the tree, staring off into space. "Excuse me, Tenny," Caitlin said, and she headed in the boy's direction.

It wasn't until she was almost at his feet that Jed noticed her. "Jed, I'm so sorry about what happened," Caitlin began.

Without looking up, he pulled up a handful of grass and tossed it back on the ground. "It's not fair, Caitlin. It was an accident. They've got to realize that."

"How's Ian?" she asked, sitting down.

"I'm not allowed to tell anyone. Emily isn't, either."

Caitlin gasped. "He's not going to die!"

Jed shook his head. "No, I guess I can tell you he's going to live. But right now he's a very sick boy."

"So the rumors about the coma are true." Caitlin felt ill.

"It was a freak accident," Jed said, his eyes pleading with her to believe him. "Diana ran inside to answer the doorbell. It was a salesman, and she tried to get rid of him as soon as she could. But just as he was leaving the phone rang. It was an emergency call for Dr. Foster. Diana had to locate him, and that took a few minutes. By the time she got back to Ian, he was lying unconscious on the steps."

"That's terrible," she said. "How's Diana? She must feel so awful."

Jed shrugged. "You can't imagine how hard she's taking it. I haven't seen her since she went home. Her parents won't let Emily or me talk to her."

"Is she ever coming back?"

146

"No. I'll probably never see her again." Tears were forming in his eyes. "I should have been there with her."

"You weren't?" Caitlin asked, surprised.

He shook his head. "I was supposed to be at the rehearsal, remember? But I was going to stop off at the Fosters' for a while beforehand. Instead, I got caught up in my biology project and didn't make it anywhere." He tried a weak smile. "How'd the show go?"

"Oh, fine, but that's not important now," Caitlin said. "Poor Diana. It could have happened to anyone."

"You sound as if you really mean that," Jed said. "And I thought you didn't like her."

"I didn't know her very well." Feeling strangely uneasy, Caitlin got up. "Take care of yourself, Jed. I've got to run to class."

She'd won. At last Diana was no longer a threat to her. But why wasn't she enjoying her victory? Somehow she didn't feel as good as she had expected to feel. Nothing seemed to matter to her now except the condition of Ian Foster. She turned her mind to the weekend. Saturday was her birthday, and she was going home to Ryan Acres. At least there was something to look forward to.

The heavy sheets of rain battering the windows and french doors of the breakfast room at her grandmother's estate did little to lift Caitlin's spirits. Instead of waking up to a chorus of "Happy Birthday" and coming down to find a room draped with crepe paper and balloons, she was greeted with nothing. She was all alone.

She'd arrived home the night before to an empty house. Not only wasn't her grandmother there, but the note advising Caitlin that she was in Washington for the weekend visiting friends said nothing at all about Caitlin's birthday. As if that weren't bad enough, Caitlin was coming down with a cold. Her throat was scratchy, and she felt feverish.

Caitlin wiped a tear of self-pity from her eye. What was her birthday, anyway? Just another day in the year. Desperately she tried to convince herself that it didn't matter, but the truth was that she felt forgotten and alone.

She walked listlessly across the room to the round oak table where one lonely place was set. She sat down. A lovely arrangement of hothouse flowers decorated the center of the table, but it failed to cheer Caitlin.

As she withdrew the white linen napkin from its silver holder and shook it over her lap, Catherine, another of the servants, entered the room with a tray in her hands.

"Good morning, miss."

Caitlin couldn't help noticing that the weather must have been affecting the maid's usual good spirits, too. Her expression was dour as she set her tray on the sideboard, then placed a plate of poached eggs in front of Caitlin. A moment later she returned with a glass of juice and the morning newspaper, then left.

After breaking her eggs with her fork tip and spreading them over the toast, Caitlin picked up the paper. Out of boredom, she scanned the front page headline: "Headmaster's Son Poisoned Accidentally."

Almost against her will, her eyes moved down to the smaller print.

Following an investigation into the mysterious injury of Ian Foster last Friday, a report has been released today by the medical examiner indicating that the six-year-old boy had ingested a small quantity of a poisonous chemical just prior to his arrival at Roanoke Hospital by ambulance. Ian, son of Dr. and Mrs. Richard Foster, had been under the care of a baby-sitter when the accident occurred. The boy remains in serious condition at the hospital, paralyzed from the waist down.

Police reports indicate that the child apparently entered a maintenance shed on the Fosters' grounds and ate some pesticide, which had recently been delivered there. The baby-sitter, a student at Highgate Academy where Dr. Foster is headmaster, found the child unconscious on the back steps. By the time . . .

The paper fell from Caitlin's hands as scenes of the afternoon of Ian's accident flashed in front of her eyes: the locked shed door . . . the key she'd hung back up . . . her aggravation and her hasty departure . . the door she'd kicked shut behind her—unlocked.

No! She couldn't bear those thoughts!

With a muffled cry, she pushed her chair roughly from the table. She couldn't think about it! She couldn't allow the truth to sink in!

Caitlin rushed from the room, down the back hall, and out into the pouring rain. Her feet flew across the sodden lawns as she made her way to the stables.

She had to escape! She couldn't let the awful realizations catch up to her! Immediately she went to Challenger's stall. Forcing herself to think only of the task at hand, she threw a saddle on his back and a bridle over his head. Grabbing a rain slicker from the wall, she pulled it on and hurried Challenger toward the stable exit.

She'd already dragged the reluctant animal into the downpour when Jeff, the stable hand, came rushing out of his room at the end of the barn.

"Miss Ryan! What are you doing?"

"I'm going riding." Her voice was deathly flat.

"In this weather? Are you crazy? The ring's a pool of mud."

"I'm not going into the ring. I'm going out on the trails."

"You're out of your mind," Jeff said. He reached for the bridle, but Caitlin thrust his hand away. Her eyes were blazing.

"Don't try to stop me," she cried. "You can tell my grandmother whatever you like. She couldn't even remember it was my birthday today!"

Caitlin yanked Challenger out into the muddy yard and vaulted into the saddle. She heeled the spirited horse forward. Disoriented by the driving rain, he snorted and reared up. With a sure pressure of her hands and legs, Caitlin brought him down and set him moving away, his pounding hooves sending up a spray of mud.

She was oblivious to the pelting raindrops as she drove Challenger down a dirt track. The bare branches of the trees on either side of the track lashed at Caitlin. The horse pranced in rebellion at the cold, lancing rain and tried to take the bit in his teeth. The reins firm in her hands, Caitlin maintained control, turning him into the brown and barren open meadow.

They raced over the fields as one. In the cold air a mist of steam rose from the horse's heated body. Rivulets of icy water ran off Caitlin's slicker into her eyes and down her neck, but she noticed none of it. Her only thought was that if she could ride hard enough, long enough, she could forget.

Yet the dark thoughts continued to race through her mind. *I was the one responsible—I, Caitlin. Ian could have died because of me.*

She leaned closer over Challenger's neck. The wind blew the hood of her slicker off her head. Death. Always death. She couldn't bear it again. Her own mother was dead because of her. Her grandmother would never forgive her for that.

Of course! It made sense to her now why her grandmother had forgotten her birthday, why she never took any joy in celebrating it. Her birthday was also the anniversary of her mother's death. No wonder her grandmother didn't want to be with her that day.

I never should have been born, Caitlin thought bitterly. *All I do is bring misery to people. Now, because of my carelessness, Ian is paralyzed for the rest of his life!*

Caitlin pushed Challenger faster—and at that moment she didn't care if she ever came back.

*　*　*

Two hours later, when Challenger clopped through the mud to the stable door, Caitlin was draped inertly over his neck. Her hair was soaked and clinging to her head; her hands still held the reins only because she'd looped them around her fingers.

Jeff was waiting for her, his face drained by anxiety. But Caitlin didn't notice. She raised her head only slightly as he grabbed Challenger's bridle and led the two of them inside. He tied the horse, then quickly reached up for the girl.

"My God," he whispered under his breath as he dragged the limp, wet girl down. "Let go of the reins, Miss Ryan. Let go. You're home."

Her fingers gradually released their grip.

"What have you done," he said softly.

As her feet touched the stable floor, she roused briefly and reacted to his words. "Challenger will be fine. Just walk him for a while."

"I'm not worried about the horse. It's you!" He grabbed her as she began to sway, then led her to a bench beside the stalls. "You're soaked to the skin and shivering! Let me get you a blanket."

As he rushed away, Caitlin tried weakly to push the wet tendrils of her hair from her eyes. Her cheeks felt hot even to her own hand. A sudden chill shook her body, and she welcomed the warmth of the cool blanket Jeff wrapped tightly around her.

"I've got to get you to the house. Do you think you can walk? Or should I carry you?"

Caitlin refused to admit how rubbery her legs felt when Jeff helped her stand. It took all her effort to force her feet to move as Jeff, with one arm supporting her and the other holding an umbrella, helped her out of the stable and across the distance to the house.

As they entered the back door, Catherine was coming down the hall with a pile of laundry in her arms. She took one look at Caitlin and dropped the laundry on the floor, then rushed forward. "What in heaven—!"

"She went out riding," Jeff responded. "I tried to stop her, but she took off like a rocket. She said something about Mrs. Ryan forgetting her birthday."

"My, my," Catherine clucked. "Let me get her out of those things and into a hot bath. Whatever did you get into your head, Miss Caitlin? Riding on a day like this?"

"I'll be all right, Catherine"—Caitlin forced out the words through chattering teeth—"once I get a bath."

"You'll be lucky if you don't get more than that," Catherine scolded with motherly concern. Together, she and Jeff helped Caitlin down the hall to the foot of the stairs.

"I can get up myself," Caitlin said stubbornly. But as she reached out a hand for the bannister, the world suddenly spun into dizzy darkness, and she collapsed into Jeff's arms.

16

"So, you're feeling better." Five days later, Regina Ryan laid a hand on her granddaughter's brow and nodded. "Yes, the fever's down at last. It's a wonder you didn't kill yourself and the horse. Whatever made you want to go riding out in that storm?"

Caitlin remained mute, a feeling of bitter despair rising up inside her. What good would it do, she thought, to tell her grandmother the truth about why she had taken that ride?

Regina walked across the bedroom toward the windows and rearranged the vase of flowers set on the table between them. "I had the gardener send these up for you from the greenhouse."

"Thank you," Caitlin said quietly. "They're beautiful."

"Yes, I have always liked yellow roses myself." Adjusting the sleeves of her gray silk suit, Regina turned back toward Caitlin. "Catherine and Jeff have hinted to me about the reason for your mad ride. Really, Caitlin, I wonder at your sense sometimes. You know I often have to sacrifice my personal life for business. The friends I visited in Washington are very much involved in the political interests of the mining industry. Their goodwill is essential. I couldn't have refused their invitation simply because it was my granddaughter's birthday."

"But it was my *sixteenth* birthday," Caitlin managed to mumble through tears. Better to let her grandmother believe that that was the only reason for her misery.

"You would have gotten your gift and cake on my return. I've never ignored your birthday, although I have always failed to understand the fuss you make over it. You'd better watch yourself, or you will become as irresponsible and self-serving as your father was! Well, I hope your carelessness has taught you a lesson." She paused at the foot of Caitlin's bed. "Several of your friends have called to see how you are. If you're feeling strong enough, you may call Ginny at the dorm this evening. I'll have Catherine bring up the cards you've received."

"I'll call Ginny later," Caitlin said weakly.

Her grandmother started toward the door. "Rest, then. The doctor will be here again in the morning, though I would guess you'll have to remain in bed for another week. I'll stop in later. If you feel well enough this evening, Catherine will bring up your gifts and your cake." And with that, Regina left the room, closing the door softly behind her.

Caitlin turned her cheek into the pillow and

closed her tear-filled eyes. She'd received not one word of sympathy or understanding. Instead she'd gotten a lecture. She wondered if it would have made a difference to her grandmother if she had died.

The thoughts that had been plaguing her during the days she'd tossed in feverish sleep slowly overwhelmed her again. *She* was responsible for Ian Foster's paralysis. The mere thought made her want to slide back into unconsciousness again.

There was a light knock on the door, and Catherine came in quietly. "I've brought you some mail. You'll probably feel better reading it. How about some fresh orange juice? I'll bring up a pitcher." As the maid ministered to her, Caitlin picked up the envelopes she'd placed on the bed cover. There were more than a dozen. *At least somebody cares about me*, Caitlin thought miserably. She glanced at the envelopes, all neatly slit open. She recognized one in Ginny's handwriting and slowly drew out the card.

There was a handwritten note from Ginny scratched inside the humorous get-well card. Caitlin read it quickly, then folded the card and sighed as she dropped it in her lap.

Ginny had written that the word going around was that Diana had transferred to an out-of-state school but that her exact location was being kept a secret. Not even Jed or Emily knew where she'd gone.

For the first time, Caitlin could understand the pain Diana was probably suffering. But she couldn't think about it now, she couldn't think of any of it! Short of admitting her guilt, there was nothing she could do. And there was no point in confessing. Diana was gone and could make a new life for herself. And nothing could undo Ian's paralysis. It wasn't as though Caitlin's admitting the truth would change anything. And she just couldn't bear any more pain. Why should she open it all up again? She wouldn't have to lie. All she had to do was remain quiet and wait. Eventually people would forget about the tragedy. Eventually her pain would subside.

Yet in the week that followed, as Caitlin regained her strength, she was attacked by stabbing pricks of conscience. She pushed them away as well as she could and tried to turn her thoughts to other things—anything not connected with Ian's accident.

Caitlin returned to Highgate right after Thanksgiving break. Her spirits were raised by the expressions of concern she got from her friends. Ginny even threw her a surprise belated birthday party.

Caitlin realized she truly had been missed. It helped to quiet some of the pain—that is, until she saw Jed again, in the hall after her math class.

He was as handsome as ever, standing out like a jewel in the crowd of students in the corridor, but he looked tired and strained. It was clear that the ordeal had taken its toll on him too.

Just looking at him, Caitlin felt the pain rising once again. The old yearnings, the jealousy, the rejection, and the terrible agony of her guilt overwhelmed her. The only way to get rid of the pain, she realized, was to avoid Jed. Quickly she looked down at the books in her arms so that when Jed passed, there was no need to acknowledge him. She didn't know if he'd seen her, and she didn't want to know. Not now.

Soon Caitlin settled back into the old and familiar routine of the school. Few mentions were made of either Diana or the accident. While she'd been sick, the soccer team had taken the "C" league state championship. Ginny had won the fall horse show. Talk had shifted to plans for the Christmas break: Gloria was going skiing in the Alps; Morgan to her parents' winter home in Palm Beach; Ginny to her family in Petersburg. Jed, of course, was going home to Montana.

"I wish you weren't going home for Christmas," Caitlin told Ginny one morning as they were getting dressed.

Ginny laughed. "Why not? We always have such great Christmases."

"If you weren't going home, you could spend Christmas with me."

"Why don't you ask someone else?"

"Who? I don't have another friend I get along with as well as I do with you." She sighed. "I'm beginning to hate holidays."

"Don't be silly! You just haven't gotten over your illness yet, so you're depressed."

Caitlin shrugged. "Yeah, I guess."

"There's the big Christmas party in the boys' dorm this Friday. That ought to cheer you up."

"I don't know. I haven't felt like partying much lately."

"Come on! It'll do you good to get out." Ginny studied her friend. "Look, I know you're still upset about your grandmother forgetting your birthday, but don't let her get to you! That's just the way she is. She doesn't know how to show affection."

"Maybe." Caitlin hadn't told anyone—not even Ginny—the real reason for her ride that rainy day. Still, she felt better for her friend's sympathy.

"You're coming," Ginny finally said firmly, "even if I have to drag you there."

"Okay, okay," Caitlin relented, "but I may leave early."

The girls dressed with care that Friday night. For Caitlin it was a matter of habit to take pains with her appearance, but Ginny usually dressed simply and never took much time getting ready.

"What's this?" Caitlin teased as she watched her friend fuss with her hair in front of the mirror. "I know, Bert's going to be there tonight!"

Ginny grunted noncommittally. "I figured it wouldn't hurt to wear my hair a new way."

"Ha! Guess I'll have to keep an eye on you tonight."

"That'll be a nice change."

Caitlin laughed.

As they entered the boys' dorm building, where the party was being held, Caitlin stayed at Ginny's side instead of heading off to circulate through the crowd as she had always done in the past. Most of the downstairs rooms were in use—the two lounges, the library, the huge recreation room where the band was playing, and several smaller rooms. It seemed as though nearly everyone at Highgate was there. Caitlin didn't see Jed, however, and she sighed in relief. She didn't feel ready to face him just yet.

She waved to Dorothy and Brett and saw Emily and Terry dancing. Then Roger and Tim came over to greet them.

"Hey, glad you guys are here." Roger grinned. "Some party, huh?"

They had trouble hearing him over the blare of music. He saw Caitlin looking in the direction of the band and leaned over and yelled in her ear. "Let's dance." Roger and Gloria had broken up a few weeks earlier, and Caitlin sensed he'd begun to be interested in her again.

She shook her head and shouted back, "Later."

He shrugged good-naturedly. "I'll be back." He and Tim wandered off.

Caitlin motioned to Ginny to join her in one of the quieter rooms. The two of them started walking, shouldering their way through the crowd, answering calls as they passed. When they finally reached the back room and the refreshment table, they could talk to each other without shouting.

"So, have you seen Bert?" Caitlin asked playfully.

To her surprise, Ginny nodded and pointed to the room behind them with her thumb.

"Well, why didn't you stop?" Caitlin asked. "I wouldn't have cared."

"I'm not ready yet."

"Yeah, and you probably won't be for the rest of the night." Caitlin shoved a paper cup of soda in Ginny's hand. "Come on. We'll go in there and stand at the side of the room where he can see you."

Hesitantly, Ginny allowed herself to be pulled along by Caitlin. With all the people milling around, it was almost impossible to see the comfortable couches and side tables in the student lounge. Caitlin directed Ginny to the side of the room near the bookcases.

In a moment a blush of color flooded Ginny's cheeks. Caitlin quickly turned in the direction of Ginny's gaze and saw lanky, blond-haired Bert Simpson get up from the sofa. She gently elbowed her friend, and Ginny's cheeks grew redder still.

Bert also seemed shyly embarrassed as he stepped up to them. "Hi, Ginny."

"Hi, Bert." Ginny's voice was barely audible.

"Good to see you, Bert," Caitlin said graciously. For a change there was no flirtation in her manner. "Listen, you two stay here and talk," she added nonchalantly. "I'm going to go get another soda."

Before Ginny could protest, Caitlin slipped off, chuckling to herself, happy that Ginny had found someone she liked. Caitlin moved back toward the refreshment table and left her empty cup there. She wasn't really thirsty; the soda had been an excuse. She picked up a few potato chips and was nibbling on them when Roger Wake came running up to her.

"Gotcha now. You're going to dance with me— or else." He pulled her down the hall to the recreation room and into the midst of the crowd surrounding the dance floor.

But Caitlin refused to dance. "Please, Roger, no," she said with unusual testiness. "I'm kind of tired tonight."

Roger studied her. "You *have* been looking kind of draggy lately. Sure you're feeling all right?"

Caitlin was startled by his comment. It wasn't like Roger to be very perceptive. She shrugged. "I don't know."

Just then the band switched to a slow dance. "You could manage this one," Roger suggested.

"Okay, if you insist."

Caitlin and Roger ended up staying on the floor for three more dances, until the band stopped for a break. She left Roger at the edge of the floor as Kim Verdi came up. "Hey, I've been looking for you, Caitlin. Boy, have I got something to tell you!"

"Really?" Caitlin wasn't particularly interested. The dancing had taken more out of her than she'd expected, and she felt a little shaky as she walked away with Kim. "I was just going to get a soda."

"I'll go with you. I was just talking to Jessica. You know she's been going out with Ronny. Well, guess who he showed up with tonight?"

"Who?" Caitlin asked, only half listening. Soon after she'd heard Kim out and Kim had moved on to spread her gossip elsewhere, Caitlin left the refreshment table and squeezed her way into the lounge. She wanted to find a quiet corner where she could sit and relax for a while. Ginny and Bert were still talking and appeared engrossed in each other. From there she went on into a small room that wasn't nearly as crowded as the others. The lights were dim, and there was a soft chair in the corner. Caitlin plopped into it, leaned back, and closed her eyes.

Ah, peace at last, she was thinking, when a deeply pleasant voice suddenly spoke from just beside her.

"Hello, Caitlin. You trying to get away from all the noise, too?"

Her eyes popped open, and she swung her head to the side to meet the intent gaze of Jed Michaels.

He'd pulled up a folding chair beside her and was sitting back casually, his long legs stretched out in front of him. His eyes were watching her face. "I haven't seen you in a while. I heard you've been sick."

She nodded. Her throat had tightened, but she forced herself to relax. Even so, her voice sounded husky when she spoke. "I had the flu."

"You're still pale."

"Am I?" she uttered. That he should notice threw her off guard. "You look tired yourself."

"I guess I am. After all that's gone on . . ." His voice trailed off.

Caitlin clenched her hands in her lap. She didn't feel capable of discussing the accident; in fact, she wasn't sure what to say. She felt a strange tingling in her body having Jed sitting so close. This was the last thing she'd expected to happen that evening.

"I heard you guys won the soccer championship. Congratulations. I guess you're pretty excited."

"Yeah." He smiled. "Everyone was counting on us so much, I'm glad we didn't let them down."

"It's the first time in years the team's ever gotten so far."

With the conversation on a lighter note, Caitlin chanced a look up at Jed. The light from the lamp on the wall behind them cast a shadow over his face, accenting his strong bones, his firm mouth, and the deep cleft in his chin. There was a long pause in their conversation, and Jed's expression gradually grew more serious.

"You've changed." He spoke almost as though he were talking to himself.

Caitlin was startled, and her voice caught in her throat.

"I can't put my finger on it," he continued thoughtfully, "but this is the last place I'd have expected to find you."

"This party?"

"No, sitting here by yourself. You're usually out there in the middle of everything with five guys after you. Maybe I misjudged you."

"Misjudged me?" Caitlin felt so light-headed, she was unable to utter more than a few words.

"I had you pegged as a party girl, a flirt. I've had that picture of you so stuck in my head, I never looked to see if that was really you."

"I see." Caitlin couldn't keep the frostiness from her voice.

"Don't get angry. I'm not trying to insult you." Jed sat up a little straighter in the chair, rested his elbow on his thigh, and propped his chin on his closed fist. "Maybe I shouldn't be telling you this, but I was real sure that weekend at your grandmother's that you were trying to split Diana and me up."

Stunned, Caitlin looked at him. She didn't know what to say. She'd waited so long for Jed to show some interest in her, but now that he was, she wanted to bolt and run away. She was afraid of the tension building inside her, afraid that it meant she was still attracted to him. And yet she couldn't be—not after everything that had happened.

"Look." He sighed. "This mess with the accident has really taken a toll on me. I have no idea where Diana is now. She's made it pretty clear she wants nothing further to do with anyone from Highgate. Whether that's her parents' decision or hers, I don't know. I worry about her, but breaking her ties here was probably the best thing she could do."

"It would have been hard for her to come back."

"Yeah." He shook his head. "Well, I didn't come to cry on your shoulder. I saw you over here by yourself and thought maybe it was time we got to know each other again." Suddenly he grinned, reached out a hand, and patted her shoulder. "I'm glad we talked."

Caitlin couldn't believe the thrill that went through her at the light touch of his hand. "Yes . . . I am, too."

"I'm going to head home and get some sleep." He started to rise. "Maybe we can get together sometime after Christmas break." His eyes caught hers for a long moment, and Caitlin felt as though she were being hypnotized. All she could do was nod her head quickly.

"I'll see you then." His voice held a soft promise.

"Yes," she whispered. And he turned and walked away.

17

"I don't know what to make of it, Ginny." Caitlin confided her confusion as the two girls walked back to their dorm later that evening. "Jed came over to talk to me and was so nice. He even hinted about going out after the Christmas break."

"That's interesting." Ginny was glowing. Her evening with Bert had gone rather well, too.

"I don't understand it. Why is he being so nice to me?"

"You, of all people, asking that question?" Ginny said with amazement. "When has your ego ever been shaky?" She paused and frowned. "But I guess I'm kind of surprised, too. I had the impression Jed was really upset about Diana and everything."

"He is. He said as much."

"Well, maybe he wanted someone to talk to," Ginny said reasonably.

"That's probably it." Caitlin let the subject drop. What was the point of pursuing it? Ginny had no more insight into Jed's behavior than Caitlin did, and as much as she was drawn to Jed, perhaps it was better to forget about him. He brought too many unpleasant reminders with him.

Yet one evening a few days after they'd gotten back from Christmas break, Caitlin got a call on the dorm telephone.

"Hi, Caitlin. It's Jed."

"Jed . . . oh, hi, how are you?"

"Pretty good."

"Did you have a nice Christmas? It must have been great getting back to Montana and seeing your family."

"Yeah, it was. I didn't realize how much I'd missed the ranch—or how much they missed me." He laughed. "How was your holiday?"

"Okay." Caitlin didn't want to talk about the deadly quiet celebration of Ryan Acres: she and her grandmother had sat at opposite ends of the huge, formally set dining room table for Christmas dinner, and afterward, there had been almost a regimented gift opening beside the tree in the grand living room. The whole day had been refined and stiff and unwelcoming. She'd spent her New Year's alone, too, as her grandmother had gone off to an adults-only party at a neighboring estate. "It was just my grandmother and me, but it was nice," she fibbed.

He paused. "I was wondering if you'd like to go riding with me after classes tomorrow."

For an instant Caitlin's mind went blank with surprise. "Well, yes . . . I mean, no, I'm not busy."

"Great." She could almost see his lazy grin over

the phone wires. "I'll meet you at the stables at three. Think I'll have any trouble getting a decent horse, or should I run down at lunch and reserve one?"

"At this time of year you can have your pick."

"Then I'll see you tomorrow, Caitlin."

"Yes, see you."

The line went dead, and after a moment of staring dazed at the wall, she hung up the receiver.

When she got back to the room, she sat on the edge of her bed like a zombie. Ginny looked up from her homework and studied her.

"Caitlin, what's wrong with you?"

"You won't believe this, Ginny, but that phone call was from Jed. He asked me to go riding with him tomorrow."

"What do you know?" Ginny eyed Caitlin speculatively. "Are you going?"

"I said I would."

"It makes me wonder. You've really been avoiding him. Even I almost believed you weren't interested anymore. He must like the challenge."

"You make it sound so calculating!"

"No, neither of you planned it this way. Just think, Caitlin"—Ginny couldn't resist teasing her friend a little—"if you'd played hard-to-get right from the beginning, you would have saved yourself a lot of trouble."

Jed was waiting when Caitlin arrived at the stables. It was a little after three, but she was enough of her old self not to be ready for a date on time. Besides, she'd taken extra care with her appearance and knew she looked superb in her white cable-knit sweater under a violet down vest. Beige-toned stretch riding pants clung to her shapely legs, as did her gleaming black leather hunt boots. Her long hair was drawn back in a thick braid under her velvet hard hat, and the brisk air had brought rosy color to her cheeks.

Jed was waiting with Duster and his stable mount already tacked as she entered the paddock. He led them out through the gate. "A little nippy, but it should feel good once we get riding." His old, familiar smile greeted her.

"It'll keep the horses spunky. Hi, there, Duster. Yes, you're a good boy." She handed the horse his usual sugar cube, then spoke to Jed. She felt a bit self-conscious. "Have you been riding since the last time we all went out together?"

"A few times, but not as often as I've wanted to. I'll manage to stay aboard, if that worries you." He laughed.

"I wasn't worried about that. You're a fantastic rider."

"I don't know about 'fantastic.'"

Caitlin glanced down from his penetrating eyes and fiddled with her stirrups. "Where did you want to go?"

"The trails, I guess, for starters. I need to get my legs back in shape."

Caitlin might have commented that his legs, in tight jeans, looked in good shape to her, but that wasn't the kind of flirtatious comment she could make to Jed Michaels. Especially not now.

As Caitlin mounted and began adjusting the stirrups, Jed called out, "Ready?"

She nodded quickly, and they headed off away from the barn. The sky was clear, the air fresh and cold but invigorating. The horses' iron-shod hooves made a clicking noise on the semifrozen ground, and both animals snorted, glad to be out and moving.

Jed and Caitlin rode silently for a while, but it was a comfortable silence, and it gave Caitlin a chance to study Jed. Again she was impressed with his ease in the saddle. His legs were tight, his heels down; he moved with the horse and controlled it effortlessly. But as she looked at Jed, all the old feelings that she'd been trying to forget came rushing back. She tried very hard to suppress them.

"Let's cut off across this field," she suggested suddenly. "We can open them up to a canter on the grass. There's a fence at the end of the field. If we jump it, we can connect with the south trail up over the hill."

He glanced quickly at her, then lifted his shoulders and said, "Why not?"

She felt so full of bound-up tension that she needed a faster pace, a bit of excitement, to relieve it. They matched strides as they set the horses over the grassy pasture, but the fence wasn't wide enough for them to jump abreast. Jed hung back, and Caitlin heeled Duster forward and over cleanly. She looked back quickly over her shoulder to see Jed flying over the fence in perfect form. They cantered up the trail a few minutes longer, then Jed pulled his horse down to a walk, and Caitlin followed suit.

"Do you mind the slower pace?" he asked. "I thought we could talk and look at the scenery."

"Fine with me. There's a beautiful view from the top of this hill."

"I thought you'd like to know that Emily was saying some nice things about you the other day. She told me how glad she was that you'd gotten her involved in the fund-raiser. She's made some new friends, and that really helps with Diana gone and all."

"Everybody likes her."

"You know," he said thoughtfully, "that's another thing I didn't give you credit for. I probably shouldn't tell you this, but I thought you had an ulterior motive for getting friendly with her."

Caitlin flinched inwardly. Jed had no idea how close to the truth he was, but she didn't let her uneasiness show. She deftly changed the subject away from herself. "Tell me about your ranch. You've never told me too much about it."

"Haven't I? Seems to me I've bored a lot of people with the details. What do you want to know?"

"Oh, what it's like living in the West with all those wide-open spaces."

"Different from here, that's for sure. There's a real sense of being in touch with the land. Apart from the ranch hands, you don't see a lot of people. The nearest town of any size is twenty miles away, and we only drive in twice a week at the most."

"You're that far out?"

He laughed. "We thought we were fairly close in. Some of the ranchers are more than fifty miles from the nearest town."

"You must feel hemmed in here."

"Oh, once in a while, but I like the change. It's good to see how the rest of the world is doing."

"Do you actually herd cattle with horses still, or is that just in the movies?"

"Some of the work is done with horses, although a lot of ranchers are using Jeeps and helicopters. My father uses all of them. He thinks of himself as progressive. . . ."

Caitlin listened with interest as Jed continued talking. "Your ranch house sounds beautiful," she commented as he paused in his description of his home.

"It's nice. My father built the house himself and takes a lot of pride in it, but it's certainly not in the same class as your grandmother's place."

"Are you saying Ryan Acres is ostentatious?" She lifted her chin in feigned offense.

"Let's just say it suits your grandmother." He chuckled.

"You'd make a good politician."

"I've been told that before." He pulled his horse to a stop. "Let's walk for a while. Do you mind?"

"No. In fact, there's a rock we can climb up ahead where there's an incredible view."

They tied the horses' reins to a sturdy tree branch and with Caitlin directing the way, set out on foot the rest of the way up the hillside.

"When we get to the top, you'll be able to see all the way over into West Virginia," Caitlin instructed.

They lapsed into a comfortable silence as they picked their way up the path to the observation point Caitlin had promised.

"See." She pointed. "Those mountains over there are West Virginia. My grandmother's mines are just beyond them."

In the clear air the visibility was wonderful, and for several moments they stood side by side looking around quietly.

Caitlin turned toward Jed, then stopped short as she saw the expression on his face. He was less than a foot away. His eyes were luminous and soft, and she felt his gaze almost as a physical touch. Her breath caught in her throat.

"Caitlin," he said quietly, "I've been thinking . . . I'm wondering what you're thinking. Here I was telling you how much I cared for Diana. I stopped going out with her only because I had no choice. And now I'm here with you. All I can think is that I want to see more of you."

"I—wasn't thinking anything." Caitlin was breathless with surprise. "I thought you were looking for friendship, and—and Diana's gone, and . . ." She could think of nothing else to say.

"Yes, she's gone, and I've been thinking about my feelings for her, too. At first I thought there was something wrong with me for not missing her more. Then I began to realize that what I felt for her—had felt for her all along—was what I would have felt for a sister. I loved her, but in a brotherly way. She reminded me of my real sister—shy, unsophisticated, out of her depth at Highgate." He paused. "A couple of years ago my parents were divorced, and my sister took it real hard. I was the only one she felt she could turn to, the only person she felt she still could trust. I've begun to realize that I was acting the same way with Diana. Not that I didn't sincerely care about her." His eyes had never left Caitlin's face. "Do you understand what I'm saying?"

"Yes, I think so." Caitlin spoke the words, though in truth she could barely believe what she was hearing. It seemed more like a dream. Jed was saying the very things she'd wished to hear him say for so long. She felt dizzy with joy.

"Are you all right?" He reached his hand out to gently grip her upper arm. "Maybe I shouldn't have said this."

"No. I'm glad. It's fine. I just didn't expect—I had no idea you felt the way you do."

"I was kind of surprised myself when I realized. I've been attracted to you right from the start. That day I met you in the hall, I said to myself, 'Wow, there's a girl I want to get to know.' But then I started getting the impression you were just a flirt. I can't stand girls like that. My mother was like that, and I'll never forgive her for what she did to my father."

"I'm sorry."

He shrugged. "That's in the past. I've learned to live with it."

His hand still rested on her arm, but now his

fingers closed around it, and he slowly pulled her toward him. She stared up into his eyes, mesmerized, as he drew her closer. She felt delightfully lightheaded to be so near to him.

She felt his other hand go around her waist, and then he was bending toward her. He smiled softly and whispered, "I've been wanting to do this all afternoon."

He was so close, she felt the soft brush of his breath on her cheek. Then, in the next moment, his mouth was covering hers, gently, warmly, sweetly. All thoughts were swept from Caitlin's mind as she responded to the surging thrill she felt inside her. Never had a kiss felt like this before; never had she felt so dizzy, so alive! She leaned closer to him, and he hugged her tightly against his chest. She wanted the kiss to go on forever, and almost protested aloud when a moment later he slowly drew away.

Again he stared down at her, then heaving a sigh, pulled her back and laid his cheek against the silky softness of her hair. "Oh, Caitlin," he whispered, "this is just the beginning."

"Yes," she breathed against his chest, "the beginning."

18

"I don't know which was worse," Ginny told Caitlin three months later, "the sourpuss you were awhile back or the lovesick puppy you are now."

Caitlin had been sitting at her desk, staring into space, daydreaming. At Ginny's words she smiled and turned slightly in her seat. "Oh, this me is infinitely better."

"Aren't you nervous about this weekend?" Ginny was busy packing in preparation for going to her parents for a visit.

"No," Caitlin said, shaking her head. "Jed's already met Grandmother. It's not as if I'm bringing him home for the first time."

"But the last time around he wasn't your boyfriend." Ginny glanced at her watch. "If you plan on meeting him on time, you'd better stop daydreaming and start packing."

"What time is it?" Caitlin said, suddenly alarmed.

"Quarter to four."

"You're kidding!" She jumped up from the chair

and pulled her canvas bag out from under the bed. "Rollins will be here in a few minutes." Going to the dresser, she yanked open one of the drawers and began rummaging through its contents. "I don't need much, but I wanted to bring that new purple sweater . . . the color's so good on me. Help me find it, please?"

"Sorry," Ginny said, looking up from her suitcase. "I'm in a hurry, too. Bert's taking me to the train."

"I'll bet you're going to miss him."

Ginny nodded, her face beginning to flush a little. "He's the best thing that ever happened to me."

"I think you've got it backward. You're the best thing that ever happened to him." Caitlin stood, triumphantly holding up the turtleneck sweater. "I found it."

She finished packing her case and zipped it shut. Then she went to the mirror to brush her hair and touch up her cheeks with blusher.

Ginny, too, had finished her packing. "You ready to go? I'll walk down with you. I'm meeting Bert at the main building."

"Yeah." Caitlin glanced quickly around the room to see if she'd missed anything. "I think I'm done. Let's go."

As they hurried down the stairs, one behind the other, Jed stepped into the hall from the lounge and looked up at them. He gave them both a wide smile, but his eyes were all for Caitlin, and they shared a secret look.

Caitlin walked to his side, and he reached out an

arm to give her a squeeze. "You're looking great," he said.

"You don't look bad yourself," she responded.

"I have to make the proper impression on your grandmother."

Rollins was waiting when they arrived at the main building, so there wasn't any time to talk further to Ginny. As she got into the car, Caitlin waved to her friend. "Have a good weekend!"

"You, too, Caitlin."

Jed slid in beside Caitlin, and as Rollins closed the door, Jed leaned over to whisper in her ear, "I wonder if Rollins will miss my company up front this trip."

Caitlin put her arm through his. "Too bad if he does, because he can't have you. I'm claiming you for now"—she glanced up at him from the corner of her eye—"and then some."

Drawing her a little closer, he pressed his hand over hers. "I'd kiss you for that, but we don't want to upset Rollins."

They arrived at the house, and after greeting Margaret in the front hall and learning that Mrs. Ryan wouldn't be home until dinner, they went immediately up to their rooms.

"I'll meet you at the stables in ten minutes," Caitlin called as Jed paused before his bedroom. "You remember how to get there?"

"I do. See you there."

For the next hour and a half, they rode around the winding trails of Ryan Acres, enjoying being out in the fresh air and savoring the freedom of being away from Highgate.

"So what should I expect from your grandmother tonight?" Jed asked as they walked back to the house holding hands.

"You seemed to know exactly how to handle her last time you were here."

Jed's eyes twinkled. "But things were a little different then—I wasn't her granddaughter's date."

"Don't worry about it. Use that marvelous charm of yours, and everything will go just fine." Suddenly Caitlin glanced up at him. "You don't mean to tell me you're nervous?"

"Maybe a little," he admitted.

"I don't believe it!" Caitlin laughed. Then picking up their speed, they jogged the rest of the way to the house.

But Mrs. Ryan wasn't in the best of spirits that evening as they sat down to eat. They were dressed for dinner: Jed in a light wool sports jacket and Caitlin and her grandmother in stylish dresses. The diamond bracelet on Regina Ryan's wrist glittered as she shook out her napkin angrily. She'd had some problems at the mining office and was furious.

"These environmental fools," she raged as Catherine began serving them the first course of Chesapeake oysters in wine sauce. "I'd like to have them all thrown behind bars. All they want to do is put a thousand restrictions on my getting the ore."

"What did they do now?" Caitlin asked, trying to seem interested. It wasn't the first time she'd heard her grandmother rail against the small environmental group that periodically picketed Ryan Mining.

"They tried to close down number two. The workers got through, but we lost a good half day with all the confusion."

"I'm sorry."

"What exactly are they protesting, Mrs. Ryan?" Jed asked politely.

"Why the strip mining, of course. But I've yet to hear them suggest any other way to mine economically."

"Not that I'm taking any sides in the issue," Jed said diplomatically, "but they do have a point. I've seen the results of strip mining in other areas of the country, and it's not pretty."

"And what do you know about mining, young man?"

"Why, very little, admittedly."

"Then I would suggest you learn more on the subject before giving an opinion." Regina's voice was cool. "I always make adequate efforts to restore the land."

"My apologies." Jed smiled, turning on his charm, although Caitlin could see he was only trying to appease her grandmother. "I'm certainly not implying that you don't know how to run your business."

The ploy worked, and Mrs. Ryan's expression softened noticeably. "I didn't mean to be so sharp with you. I've had a rather frustrating day and am breaking one of my own rules by bringing my problems to the dinner table. So, tell me what has been happening at Highgate?"

"Not too much," Caitlin responded. "Spring sports are beginning to start up."

"Are you going out for the tennis team this year?"

"Sure. I wouldn't miss it. I'm going to try out for the drama club's spring play, too."

Regina frowned. "Oh, yes, I had forgotten about that silly interest of yours. Really, Caitlin, I should think you could find a better way to spend your time. This acting business isn't something you can make use of in the future."

"But I enjoy it."

"From what I hear," Jed interrupted, "she's an excellent actress. You must have seen how good she is in front of an audience at the student council fund-raiser."

"No. I'm afraid I was too busy to go." She glanced over at Jed and softened her tone somewhat. "As heir to Ryan Mining, my granddaughter will have a great deal of responsibility, and she should be preparing herself for the future. Acting won't help her at all."

From the tone of her voice, it was clear Mrs. Ryan considered the subject closed. Jed glanced at Caitlin, but her head was down. She felt humiliated that her grandmother could discuss her future as though she were a piece of furniture.

Throughout the rest of the meal, conversation stayed on a lighter note, but Caitlin couldn't wait to escape the room. She longed for the chance to talk to Jed alone, but as they rose from the table and started out into the hall, Mrs. Ryan called out. "Jed, come with me a moment. Because you seem to have some interest in mining, let me show you what we are doing at the mines. Caitlin, you may as well come along, too, although none of this is new to you."

For the next few hours, Regina Ryan showered Jed and Caitlin with details of her business and the intricacies of the mining industry. Caitlin was thoroughly bored—this was *not* the way she'd planned spending her evening with Jed. But there wasn't much she could do about it. Her grandmother would have been furious if Caitlin had dared suggest that she and Jed would rather have watched a movie.

When Mrs. Ryan finally escorted them from her study, she glanced at her watch. "It's getting late. I think it's time we all went up. I'll go with you."

At the top landing, she offered her cheek for her granddaughter's kiss. "I'll see you in the morning, my dear. Jed, I'll walk along with you. My suite is at the end of the hall here."

As Regina turned, all Caitlin had time to do was blow Jed a kiss. He blew her one, too, then followed quickly after Mrs. Ryan.

19

"What a beautiful day." Caitlin smiled up at Jed as they crossed the groomed back lawns. They'd decided after breakfast that morning to pack a lunch and take a long walk.

"Couldn't be nicer!"

He squeezed her hand a little tighter, and she rubbed her cheek lightly against his shoulder. "I'm so glad you came this weekend."

"Me, too."

They walked for a while in silence, feeling as if this delightfully sunny day had been provided especially for them. As they passed through the corner of one of the pastures, Caitlin pointed toward two mares with week-old colts at their sides.

"Look, the first foals. Aren't they adorable? Grandmother has about a dozen brood mares this year. These foals are just the beginning."

"Speaking of your grandmother"—Jed spoke more seriously—"I feel awful about last night."

"There wasn't anything you could do. My grandmother has to have her way, and if we hadn't gone to look at her mining stuff, she would have been insulted."

"I wasn't talking about that so much."

Caitlin was puzzled.

"It was the way she put you down at dinner, making such a big issue of how you spend your time, as if she has the right to tell you what to do."

"She does that all the time." Caitlin tried to appear nonchalant. "I don't think she even realizes how bad she makes me feel."

"I wish there was something I could have said."

"You tried." She looked up at him. "And I appreciate that."

They started up a low grade at the top of which was a grassy clearing scattered with early wild-flowers.

"Let's sit down here for a minute and share a Coke," Jed suggested.

"I've always liked this spot."

Finding a large patch of soft grass, they settled down side by side as Jed fished inside the knapsack for a soda, opened it, and handed it to Caitlin.

"I wish you didn't have to live in a home like this—without love," he said seriously. "What about your father's family? Have you ever considered living with them?"

"I've never heard anything about them. I—I don't know if he had a family."

"That sounds strange. Why do you use the Ryan name instead of your father's?"

"For some reason my grandmother hated my father. She won't talk about him except to say he was no good and that it's better I have her family's name."

He was watching her face. "There's something you're not telling me."

"No."

"Caitlin, I'm not trying to pry. I just don't want to see you hurt by your grandmother."

"There's nothing you or anyone else can do. My mother was her only child, and my grandmother's never forgiven me for being the cause of her death."

"I don't believe that." Jed swung around and took her by the shoulders. "Sure, she's a cold, hard lady, but she's not that cruel."

"You don't think so?" Caitlin's lips had begun to tremble. "She takes care of me because she has no choice, because providing for her orphaned grand-daughter makes her look good in other people's eyes. She's never told me she loves me; she's never even hugged me. In fact, this year she forgot my birthday! And I've been sent to a boarding school to keep me out from underfoot." Suddenly Caitlin covered her face with her hands and began to cry.

"Oh, Caitlin, I'm sorry." Jed pulled her close against his chest and gently stroked her hair. "I didn't mean to upset you."

"I—I've never told this to anyone before." Her voice was broken and barely audible.

He was silent for a minute. "Maybe it's good you finally told me. You've been holding it inside."

"I've tried so hard to make her love me. . . ."

"If only you had some other family—someone on your father's side."

"Even if I knew who he was, he doesn't want me either."

Jed gripped her a little tighter. "I thought you said your father was dead."

"I tell people that." She lifted her head and stared up at him with anguished, tear-filled eyes. "Jed, he abandoned me. After my mother died, he turned me over to my grandmother. I—I don't even know his name. . . ."

Jed lifted a hand and gently wiped the tears from her cheeks. "Oh, Caitlin," he whispered. "How could they do this to you?" For a long moment he looked deeply into her eyes, his fingers caressing her cheek. When he finally spoke, his voice was husky. "I don't want you to feel unloved anymore."

"Sometimes it's hard not to."

"But *I* love you."

Caitlin swallowed, barely believing what she was hearing. "You—you do?"

"Very much." He smiled softly. "I thought you knew."

Caitlin shook her head slowly. "I hoped you did." Everything she was feeling—the sudden joy and happiness—glowed in her moist eyes. "I love you, too. I've never felt this way before."

"And neither have I. I think about you all the time. I want to be with you, talk to you, just look at you. It feels so right, I wonder how I ever could have been happy before I got close to you." He smiled.

Caitlin lifted her hand and ran her fingers through Jed's thick hair, then traced a line down his cheek to his chin.

"Come here." He sighed.

She didn't even have time to nod as he wrapped

his arms snugly around her back and kissed her until she was breathless. She was barely aware of being slid back onto the grass until she felt the heat of Jed's body full-length against her. But it felt so good and so right to be so close to him. With his lips touching hers, speaking a message of love that words couldn't say, she allowed herself to be swept away, casting all thoughts from her mind except the love she felt for him. Never had she felt like this—never had she *wanted* to feel like this with any boy!

"Caitlin . . . you make me feel so good." His warm breath brushed against her ear.

"I love you, Jed." She let him pull her closer, and as his mouth covered hers, she was enveloped again in a dizzying cloud of happiness, until his hand slid slowly, gently over her breast and down onto the curve of her hip.

She tensed. That subtle pressure of his hand made her aware of where they were heading.

Without her saying a word, Jed leaned slightly away. "I didn't mean—"

"You don't have to apologize." She sighed. "Something happens when we start kissing."

He smiled. "We were going too fast." His eyes were hazy and his breathing heavy as he looked over at her. "But I don't want to. Not now."

Caitlin rubbed her fingers over his cheek. "A lot of guys wouldn't have stopped."

"But I'm not a lot of guys. I'm a guy who cares about you. We have lots of time, Caitlin—at least I plan on it."

"Do you?"

He nodded.

"Good." She grinned. "Because I'd like to plan on it, too."

"Would I send you back to your wicked grandmother to spend your life in misery?"

"Well, it wouldn't be that bad." She laughed.

"No, and she's not really wicked—just absorbed in her own problems. Besides, we've got all kinds of things to do together in the future. I'm going to teach you western riding and roping. I'll make you the best fence-post roper in Virginia."

"Why fence posts?"

"Because there're a lot more of them than cattle in this state, and they tend to stay in one place."

"You think I'm going to be that bad, huh?" She poked him in the ribs.

"Well, it takes practice."

"It sounds like fun." She hugged him quickly and laid her head against his chest. "I'm looking forward to it."

"If you keep hugging me like this, we're going to be in trouble again."

With that, Caitlin removed her arms from around him, sat up, and brushed off her shirt and jeans. As Jed rose, he extended his hands down to her. She gripped them, and he pulled her up beside him.

"We'll walk some more before we eat?" he asked.

She nodded.

Still holding her hands, Jed smiled and dropped a light kiss on her forehead. "I love you, Caitlin."

"And I love you."

Hand in hand, they started off across the clearing.

20

Caitlin returned to Highgate, confident in her love for Jed and truly believing that she was the happiest girl on campus. Now that she saw Jed every day, she found it difficult to remember how she had existed without him.

She was in just such a dreamy daze, thinking about Jed, when she turned a corner in a classroom building and ran straight into Emily a few days later. Both girls laughed as they knelt down to pick up their books from the floor.

"I'll bet I can guess what—or who—you were thinking about when you came around the corner." Emily grinned.

"Not hard, is it," Caitlin answered cheerfully. "So how have you been? I haven't seen you lately."

"Okay. I've decided to enter the spring horse show, and I've been busy practicing. I won't ask how you've been," she said, winking. "You and Jed have really hit it off."

"Mmmm." Caitlin sighed. "He's great."

"You don't have to tell me," Emily agreed. "Listen, I hope you know I'm happy about you and

Jed getting together. I was kind of surprised at first when he started seeing you so soon after . . . well, I guess you two were attracted to each other right from the start."

"I always thought he was cute," Caitlin said quickly, trying to block out the unmentioned name in Emily's statement. "How are you and Terry doing?" she rushed on, changing the subject.

"Absolutely fantastic!" Emily giggled.

"Great! We'll all have to go riding sometime, especially now that the weather's getting nicer."

"Sounds good." Suddenly Emily's expression clouded. "I just remembered something not so happy. I got a letter from Diana's father yesterday."

"Oh?" Caitlin swallowed hard.

"It was very short. He asked me to send along a couple of things Diana had left at my house one weekend. She's leaving the school she transferred to from Highgate. Things weren't working out for her there. Of course, he didn't say why or where she was going."

Emily shook her head. "You know, it really bothers me. I've written her tons of letters, and Jed wrote her some, too, but we've never gotten an answer. Her parents didn't even write to thank my parents for taking care of her after the accident. They had Mrs. Chaney pack up her clothes and send them. I don't know if her mother takes our letters and throws them out or if Diana really wants to cut all ties with us."

Caitlin was trying to hide the jabbing pangs of conscience Emily's words were causing. "It's sad what happened."

"Sad isn't the word. I felt so close to Diana, and

191

to have her cut me off cold, even if she is hurting—"

"Maybe, like you said, it's her parents," Caitlin interrupted.

"Yeah, maybe. Well, we'd better get going, or we'll be late for class. Listen, when is Jed bringing you out to our place for a weekend? Whatever weekend you come, I'll invite Terry, too, and we can all go riding."

"Sure! I'll talk to him." But Caitlin had to force the gaiety into her voice. All she could think about was Diana Chasen and the pain that girl had to be suffering.

She sat through French class unaware of a word Mme. Giraux said, grateful that she wasn't called on. Caitlin was thankful it was the last class of the day. Immediately afterward she went to her dorm room to be alone and try to straighten out her thoughts.

Caitlin couldn't believe how hard Emily's words had hit. She'd thought she had left all that miserable guilt behind. She'd been so sure that Diana would go away, make a new life, and that the whole incident would be forgotten.

Why did Emily have to bring it up now? Caitlin had never been so happy in her life. But if Jed knew that she was the one who had left the shed unlocked, and worse, that she had kept it a secret for so long—allowing Diana's life to be destroyed—all of Caitlin's happiness would be over.

And then what would she have? Only the terribly lonely existence in her grandmother's house. At least now she had Jed and all the love they shared. Having him made all the rest less painful. She could forget it for a while.

What she and Jed had was deep, but Caitlin had to admit it wasn't really honest. She wanted to be worthy of his love—she wanted him to believe in her completely, fully. Until she told the truth, however, she knew she wouldn't really deserve him.

Wearily she dropped her head on her arms on the desktop and sighed heavily, as if in one breath she could let out all her pain and indecision. What was she to do? Continue the lie and be sure of Jed? Or admit the truth, save another girl's sanity—and possibly lose him?

For fifteen minutes she remained still, her head on her arms, as she sought a decision. Finally she lifted her head and sat straight in the chair. She knew what she had to do. She had no choice. She had to tell Jed the truth. If she didn't, she would carry it around as a burden forever.

Pulling open the desk drawer, she quickly drew out a pad of notepaper, then fumbled in her bag for her pen. With everything in front of her, she sat a minute with closed eyes, then started writing. It was a full hour before she put down her pen and picked up the papers to read what she'd written.

Jed,

You know how very, very much I love you, but there's something I have to tell you. I'm ashamed that I haven't said this sooner, but it's been so wonderful to have you come into my life. I was afraid to tell you the truth because I might lose you.

I've just come back from talking to Emily. She told me that Diana's left the school she'd just transferred to. I feel responsible.

It goes back to the accident at the Fosters' when

Ian got into the poison. I was there that day. I went to the shed to get a prop for the fund-raiser. The door was locked. I remember having to unlock it and then hanging the key back up. But when I came out, I'd forgotten all about it being locked. I was tired and aggravated, and I kicked the door shut behind me. Ian was in the yard, but he didn't see me leaving.

It's true I hated Diana for getting you when I couldn't. It's true I did everything in my power to get you away from her. But I didn't deliberately leave that shed door unlocked. I never would have done anything like that! I just didn't think to lock it again. It was a terrible oversight.

I went back to the auditorium, where I heard the ambulance and learned that Ian had been hurt. I blamed Diana. I thought she'd been inside the house with you all that time. Besides, I was angry that everyone felt so sorry for her. I couldn't understand what it was she had that made her so well liked. I didn't tell anyone that I'd been in the Fosters' yard that day and knew she'd taken her eyes off Ian. I didn't tell anyone because I was almost sure you'd been in the house with her, and I didn't want to implicate you.

I didn't find out what really happened and learn about the poisoning until the following weekend. I was at my grandmother's, and the story was on the front page of the paper.

Once I read the article, I knew I was really to blame. I ran out of the house, got on one of the horses, and took a long ride in the pouring rain. I couldn't face the truth or admit it to myself. I wanted to die. Instead, I got sick and spent the next week in bed. I couldn't let myself think about it. It hurt too much.

By the time I came back to school, Diana was

gone for good. I thought everything would blow over. I felt weak and tired, and I still couldn't face the truth. I told myself Diana would find a new life—a good life—away from Highgate. I even avoided you because you were a reminder of the horrible secret I was keeping. Then you came to talk to me at the party. When you said you'd misjudged me, I didn't have the courage to tell you what I'd really done. I'd wanted you for so long, I just couldn't say the words.

Oh, Jed, I feel so terrible for lying to you. I want your love and respect, and I want us to stay together, but the only way I can live with myself is to tell you this. I can't stand these feelings of guilt any longer.

I know I am responsible for a lot of unhappiness and have a great debt to pay, but please tell me you'll forgive me. Please tell me you still love me!

I love you,
Caitlin

The letter said it all, but what would Jed think when he read it? Would it mean the end for them? Would he turn on her with hatred and anger? Or would he show the compassion and acceptance that had made her fall in love with him in the first place? She prayed he would understand—prayed with all her heart—but she was ready to face the consequences if he didn't. She knew she was doing the right thing. A huge burden had been taken off her mind with each word she had written.

She wouldn't be seeing Jed that night. He had a meeting with his college counselor. But the next day, sometime when they were alone, she would give him the letter.

21

Jed greeted Caitlin with a loving smile as she set her tray down beside his in the cafeteria at lunchtime the following afternoon. She put her knapsack on a chair, then sat down. Putting his arm around her shoulders, Jed hugged her quickly. "Hi, beautiful."

"Hi, handsome." Caitlin tried to keep relaxed. She didn't want Jed to know how nervous she was or that it was taking every bit of her courage to be there with him. Just seeing him and feeling his magnetism and warmth started doubts racing through her mind at the wisdom of giving him the letter.

"Boy, I'm starved," he said cheerfully. "Taking that biology exam used up all my energy."

"I'd forgotten you had a test today. How'd it go?"

"Pretty good, I think. We should get the grades on Friday."

Caitlin eyed her knapsack, which contained the neatly folded letter. But she couldn't bring herself to reach out for it just yet. *In a minute*, she told herself. She'd give it to him when they'd finished eating. She looked over at him. He was eating his sandwich, so unaware of what was about to happen.

Caitlin took a bite out of her own sandwich, but she might as well have been eating sawdust for all the pleasure she got out of it. Jed noticed her discomfort.

"What's the matter?" he said with concern. "You seem awfully quiet. Did you have a bad morning?"

"Oh, no." Caitlin jumped slightly at his words. "This morning was just fine."

"You look tired. Did you sleep all right?"

"Not bad. I went to bed early." In truth, Caitlin had tossed and turned for hours before falling asleep. "How did your meeting with Dr. Lanigan go?"

"Like I expected. We talked about some college choices, but I've got a while yet before I make any decision." He smiled. "I didn't tell him this, but I'd sure like my choice to be within traveling distance of yours."

Caitlin felt herself melting. If only she didn't have this terrible secret. She could only nod and smile.

"By the way," he said, "Emily told me about the letter she got from Mr. Chasen. She said she mentioned it to you." He frowned and shook his head. "I get so angry when I think what this mess has done to Diana's life! It was an accident. Can't anyone give her a break?"

Caitlin's face blanched at the coldness of Jed's

tone. If he was angry now, what would he say when he learned of her part in Diana's misery?

She felt his hand on her shoulder. "Caitlin, listen, don't get me wrong." He was studying her face, his green eyes suddenly worried. "I'm angry at the circumstances—not because I'm still in love with Diana."

"Jed, I—"

"I care about her, sure, but like a sister. You understand that."

She nodded. Unconsciously she reached out, and her fingers closed over her knapsack.

"And I realize she's partially to blame—she shouldn't have left Ian alone so long. But she isn't malicious. I don't think there was a hateful bone in her body."

No, Diana wasn't malicious, Caitlin thought, but she herself had been. On hearing Jed's words, she knew she couldn't give him the letter. Not with the mood he was in. That angry voice of a moment ago wouldn't be directed at a wide sweep of circumstances—it would be directed solely at her! And it wouldn't only be Jed who'd hate her—everyone else would despise her for deliberately holding back the truth for so long. She'd be an outcast.

"Caitlin." Jed leaned closer, took her chin in his fingers, and made her look at him. "Are you all right? You look upset."

"No—no, I'm not. I—I understand. You have a right to be angry, and I know you don't still love Diana. I—I just felt a little dizzy for a minute." She hated to tell another lie, but dizziness had been close enough to the truth.

Immediately Jed brought his hand up to her forehead. "You don't seem to have a fever."

"I'll be all right." She forced a smile. "I'm feeling better already. Maybe I didn't eat enough breakfast."

"Well, then, eat up. You've only taken a couple of bites out of your sandwich."

Caitlin forced herself to eat, and in a minute Jed started talking easily again. "We have to start your roping lessons soon. How about this weekend? I'm sure Aunt Ellen and Uncle Lorin would love to have you. Have you been out to their place before?"

"No, but yesterday Emily said something about us all going out there. She wanted to invite Terry."

"They've been seeing quite a bit of each other."

"I'm glad," Caitlin said. She was feeling better now that Jed had shifted the conversation away from Diana.

"You feeling okay now?" Jed studied her, and when she nodded, he smiled. "Eating something must have helped. You're not so pale now." He moved over and gave her a quick kiss.

"I hope no one saw that." Caitlin giggled. "You know the rules about kissing on campus."

"No one saw," he said assuredly, picking up the orange that was on his tray. "I've got to run. I want to stop in the library before class, but I'll see you tonight about seven."

"I'll be waiting."

"Good. Be thinking of you." He gathered up his knapsack, gave her a wink, and hurried away.

Caitlin went to her room after classes to change

into her riding clothes before meeting Ginny at the stables. As she zipped open her knapsack to get her brush, the reality of the undelivered letter caught up with her. She took it from her bag and slowly unfolded it, but she was unable to read the words of self-condemnation it contained. She felt an overwhelming urge to tear up the letter—just as she wished she could destroy every evidence of her guilt and shove the issue out of her life forever.

Yet she couldn't force her hands to tear the sheets of paper to shreds. Deep inside she knew that someday she would give the letter to Jed. He had the right to know the truth.

But now just wasn't the right time, she convinced herself. Their love for each other was still too fragile and precious. She didn't have the strength to risk losing it so quickly and to go back to the emptiness she'd known before. She needed more time to prove herself to him. Only then would she give him the letter and admit her guilt. Only when their love was secure and she could take the chance he might understand better.

She glanced at her watch and saw she only had five minutes until she was to meet Ginny. Quickly she pulled a random volume from the bookshelf above her desk. These were her personal books, and the one she chose happened to be a collection of love poems. Thrusting the letter between the pages, she returned the book, and her secret, to the shelf.

By the time Caitlin swept out the door of the dormitory, hope was back in her heart, and the smile on her face was as sparkling as the sunny day. She was herself again.

FRANCINE PASCAL

In addition to collaborating on the Broadway musical *George M!* and the nonfiction book *The Strange Case of Patty Hearst*, Francine Pascal has written an adult novel, *Save Johanna!*, and four young adult novels, *Hangin' Out with Cici*, *My First Love and Other Disasters*, *The Hand-Me-Down Kid*, and *Hats Off to Katzoff*. She is also the creator of the Sweet Valley High series. Ms. Pascal has three daughters, Jamie, Susan, and Laurie, and lives in New York City.

JOANNA CAMPBELL

As a teenager in Connecticut, Joanna Campbell was an enthusiastic reader who especially loved books about horses. An accomplished horsewoman herself, Ms. Campbell also sings and plays the piano professionally. She and her two teenaged children live in a seacoast town in Maine, where Joanna owns an antique store and writes young adult novels (many of which feature her old love, horses!).

KELLY BLAKE: TEEN MODEL

KELLY BLAKE

She's A Star

Meet 16-year-old Kelly Blake, tall and beautiful. Watch her rise in the glamorous world of high fashion. Share the excitement as Kelly is discovered and begins her career as a top model. Share her hopes and her fears as she juggles her growing career, the demands of school commitments, *and* the need for time just to be herself, Kelly Blake, sixteen, pretty, and in love with the boy next door.

Catch a Star on the Rise!
LOOK FOR:

☐ **DISCOVERED! 25638 $2.50**
KELLY BLAKE: TEEN MODEL #1

☐ **RISING STAR 25693 $2.50**
KELLY BLAKE: TEEN MODEL #2

☐ **HARD TO GET 26037 $2.50**
KELLY BLAKE: TEEN MODEL #3

☐ **HEADLINERS 26112 $2.50**
KELLY BLAKE: TEEN MODEL #4

And don't forget to watch for more KELLY BLAKE books coming soon.